THE ASSISTANT
STRONG WOMEN

TESS MOLESWORTH

Published by Tess Molesworth

tessmolesworth@gmail.com

First published 2024

Text © Tess Molesworth 2024

The moral right of Tess Molesworth to be identified as the author of this work has been asserted.

All rights reserved.

Without limiting the rights under copyright reserved above, no part of this publication may be reproduced, stored in or introduced into a retrieval system, or transmitted, in any form or by any means, without the prior written permission of both the copyright owner and the publisher of this book.

For any copyright queries, please email Tess Molesworth at tessmolesworth@gmail.com

This is a work of fiction. Names, characters, places, and incidents are either the product of the author's imagination or are used fictitiously, and any resemblance to actual persons, living or dead, business establishments, events or locales is entirely coincidental.

A catalogue record for this book is available from the National Library of Australia.

ISBN 9781763584600 (Print)

ISBN 9781763584617 (eBook)

Publishing support by Debut Books

Editorial by Stephanie Cuthbert

Cover Art & Formatting by DAZED Designs

Typesetting by Blue Wren Books

Printed by IngramSpark

For Rog!
And to those who love love.

CHAPTER 1
BLAIR

I sit at the head of the conference table, watching all my executive members dawdle in. This is not how a staff meeting should begin. I'm nearly drumming my fingers on the table top out of frustration.

It looks like they're walking into a university classroom waiting for the professor. Not members of a billion-dollar tech company.

The steam floating up from my tea is keeping me calm as I glance around the boardroom. Since I started EvaTech six years ago—when I left Silicon Valley—we've always had staff meetings at eight on a Wednesday. However, something has laxed and it's not my determination to stay at the top of the tech industry.

Everyone is looking too comfortable and casual. There doesn't seem to be any fire in their eyes. They're chatting, catching up, like members of clubs at university organising the next social function.

I stand, placing my hands on the table, and glare at all six executives.

"What the fuck is happening?" I make a point to look at each of them. "We need a new, refreshing angle, app or program. Something. I brought you to my company for ideas, innovation, not to sit on your hands scratching your arse." All of them hang their heads. Good. They should be ashamed.

Kaleb Morriss, Executive Director of Marketing, breaks the silence. It seems he always has an idea. Not always welcomed, but he was part of the initial dream and has been with EvaTech since the beginning. "I could re-brand the security app to encompass tradesmen and their companies, not just fixed businesses." A few heads come up from their slumping position to nod in agreement. "Dempsey can help with any tweaks of the code to ensure it can be applied to the area and field the tradesmen are working in."

Dempsey Sevrick, Executive for Coding and Programming had been suggested by Kaleb to join our team from the start. The two executives were part of the powerhouse that promoted EvaTech to the wider world in the beginning. More recently they've let other distractions impede on their focus at EvaTech. Dempsey began flicking through the screen in front of him. "It shouldn't be too hard. I know a few people in the trade industry. I can approach them with the current plan and discuss what changes would need to be made for an app that offers the same security the fixed companies have."

"Good. Alright, that's a start," I say, ensuring I look at all the executive members. "Those of you who have come here empty handed and without reports, let this be your warning. When we meet next you better have something from your team or I'll expect your resignation. No excuses." Turning without any further comments, I make my way to the elevators like my arse is on fire. Every businesswoman secretly knows the power of walking through corridors with the sound of her heels announcing the force and ability in motion.

EvaTech was never about making billions to retire before forty to live a life of luxury on an island. I want to continue making apps and programs that help or entertain people. I'm thirty-eight, nowhere near retirement age, and I'm sick of the stalemate.

Just as the doors begin to close a hand reaches through forcing them open again. Kaleb steps through before they are fully opened.

I'm still fuming from the inadequacy of my team right now. It hasn't been an instant brain snap. This feeling of sinking has been slowly building like a small hole in a wooden ship. Having Kaleb in this metal box with me is not helping any situation. Silence is my best friend right now. I just want to escape with my thoughts.

"I think we need to investigate Jasper," he says to the doors.

What the fuck is he talking about? Clearly, he can't read the fact that I'm too frustrated to deal with him right now.

I exhale deeply before I blow my already short fuse. "And why should I investigate my Executive Finance Officer when marketing—which is your area—is failing to bring new demographics and clients to my company? If anyone should be investigated right now, it's you."

That's it. I need out of this box. I hit the third-floor button. I originally wanted the lobby to escape this building for an hour or more. The stairs from level three will help burn through the red haze in my mind before the blinding sun can work its magic to refuel my tank.

The ding announcing the arrival of the third floor has me quickly turning to Kaleb. "You may have been with me since the beginning and are a great marketing executive, however, everyone is replaceable in my company."

The look on Kaleb's face as the doors close suggests that even I could be replaced. Am I reading too much into that look, or did Kaleb Morriss just show me his cards and EvaTech was the main feature? He can't possibly want my company. Now my mind is running that scenario around, alongside the issue of the lack of productivity that came from the staff meeting.

Redesigning an old security app? That is not enough to keep EvaTech at the top.

Staring at the closed doors, I turn onto the coding floor. People busy themselves as they see me standing at the elevator bank. The sound of fingers dancing over keyboards relaxes my heightened nerves and emotions. The calming and rhythmic taps are linked to my roots of wanting to be in technology. It's why I find myself on this floor as often as I do. Plus, the café with great tea and slices.

I've no idea why suddenly I feel like I'm drowning in an ocean. This is supposed to be my safe and happy place. I have an apartment on the west side of the city, but I spend more time here. The level where my office resides, has a home gym with a treadmill and boxing bag attached to a suite similar in size and functionality to a king-sized room in a high-end hotel.

Previously, when I've been lonely or in need of something, I've come down to the third floor and the café within—that's mainly for the coders and programmers—but everyone uses it. In times like these, when nothing new is being developed, they're continuously ensuring there are no bugs or glitches that have the potential to break EvaTech. It's calming to be on the floor that holds the productivity keeping EvaTech afloat.

Abandoning the thought of a walk, I see Juni behind the counter and it brings a much-needed smile to my face. Apart from the fact that she makes the best cup of tea, she has the kindest heart and best ears to hear all my problems.

Strolling to the counter, I'm feeling lighter with every step.

When the steam creating a cloud around the coffee machine clears, there's Juni, raising her head. "Hello, Blair," she says. She has the highly perceptive eyes of a mother. "I'll have your pot of tea ready with a collection of favourite slices. Just take a seat and I'll bring them over."

Over the years, June 'Juni' Hunter has been not just a mother figure to the young members of my company—I've watched her interact with and solve a few of their problems—but she's been there for me. With the wisdom of a woman who has lived the life of a single mother to a now-grown man, she still dotes on him and his friends. The stories she has shared have brought me closer to her and gave me a few life clarity moments that I missed out on because of my childhood.

Juni is only eight years older than my thirty-eight, which gives her more of an older sister vibe. And that's what I need today. A friend and confidant to help ease my mind with all the troubles from the executive meeting.

She brings over my pot of tea and samples of the slices I like. It's refreshing not to have had to place an order because she knows what I need. Sitting down with her own pot of tea, it seems this chat is going to take all the time needed to solve the problems.

Inhaling the steam from my tea held in my hands, I start to vent. "I've just come from the executive meeting, and I threatened everyone with their termination if they didn't come back next meeting with something to contribute to the company. Kaleb Morriss cornered me in the elevator suggesting I investigate Jasper in finance. I feel like I'm sinking." Closing my eyes I just sit with those comments floating between us.

Blowing my tea and taking a piece of caramel slice, I wait for Juni to filter through all the information. As the years have passed from me calling her, 'Mrs Hunter' out of respect for the older woman, to 'June' and finally 'Juni', I've learnt time is needed for her answer and to give me the best result. Juni is always animated when she is talking about her late husband and will regale you with amazing stories of love and early adventures in a simpler life. But when you need the professional ear and wisdom of an older lady, she chooses her words with care and precision.

"Who do you have to help you with all these things? The lack of ideas and innovation in the executive team? The overwhelming feeling of sinking? Who is with you in the boat, bailing the water?"

Juni could answer all these questions herself. I've spoken enough over the years about the sinking feeling, and she just shakes her head, waiting for me to acknowledge just how overworked I am. It's not in me to give up power. I've fought for everything that I am. I worked my arse off from less than nothing beginnings.

My mother left with any man regardless of his age provided she was getting what she needed. This left me with my father, who loved her so much he always accepted her back after she'd gone off with her latest fling. Once he knew I'd survive no matter the outcome, he took off as well. For a few years I was able to bury myself in books and technology and no one knew who was caring for me. Miss Cummins, a high school teacher, ensured my education was solid, and I could do anything I wanted. So, I picked a field that came easy to me, technology. And I made sure I would be at the top so no one could take from me.

Silicon Valley taught me it was a man's world in the tech industry and if you wanted to come out on top you had to be bigger and better than the man next to you. I managed to code and program my way to the top and gather enough money to create a nest egg and leave to start my own company.

Looking Juni in the eyes across my cup of tea with the delicious lingering taste of a caramel slice coating the inside of my mouth, I answer. "Technically I have me, myself and I to do all those things. My boat is more like a canoe, there isn't a lot of room for someone else."

She gives me a knowing look—one that only time and experience can give you.

"All boats have room for at least one more." Taking a sip of her tea and putting it down, she adds, "I think it's time. You said it yourself—you're sinking. You need an assistant and Miles would be perfect. He's young, has all the degrees—if anything he is probably overqualified. And he knows technology better than most other people."

"You've said before that he has never had a job. How do I know that he has the work ethic to last the distance at EvaTech?" There have been other times when the thought of an assistant was appealing. However, something has always prevented the idea from coming to fruition.

"If after a month he's not a fit for EvaTech, fire him. However, if he is a fit, you'll know within the month how easy it is to sail a boat with no holes." Smiling, we both look at each other and giggle.

"Now we're experts at boats, sailing and all things nautical," I say, with the first genuine smile in an age. Juni delivers smiles better than any delivery service the world over.

"It makes sense. We're bloody strong women," she says.

Juni rarely mentioned her son when we would speak in the past. When I asked her once why, her reply was one of respect. "I don't want you to think I talk to you just because my son knows about technology. So, I make our chats about my history, stories and you."

Knowing she wasn't here for her own personal gain had me respecting her more every time we chatted.

Eventually we exchanged phone numbers and she's always a classic for sending messages out of the blue and checking in with me.

Juni and I spend the remainder of our tea and slices talking about other areas of our life, although mine is mainly EvaTech related.

Sitting behind my desk, I begin to pen an acceptance letter for my Executive Assistant position starting Monday, that will only have one candidate. It needs to be professional without any hints of the secrets that were happening behind closed doors. Juni gets off in a couple of hours and she doesn't work Thursday or Friday and this letter needs to go with her.

CHAPTER 2
MILES

"Son, I love you, but you need to get up and get out of my house. You've got more degrees than people double your age. You cannot spend another week down here in my basement."

I'm twenty-six years of age, but my dear mother thinks that I can't look after myself. I've been the man of the house since my father died nearly a decade ago.

"Ma. Just leave me alone." Running my hands through my light brown, wavy hair I try not to piss my mother off too much. After all she is only saying this because she cares. I refocus back on my game—it's a waiting period for the enemy to strategise against the trap I'd set up. My buddies and I are all standing on the wall of my castle waiting for the oppositions move. I know I'm not giving Ma the attention she wants, which is adding to her irritation.

She had it tough raising a teenage boy on her own.

I wasn't sociable and I just wanted to game and escape into the gaming world with my mates. Although my father's life insurance meant that we'd been able to live practically debt free, it all took an emotional toll on her. She lost the love of her life, and I lost a role model.

Walking towards me, I see her reflection in my computer screens.

"Miles, this is an acceptance letter for an interview at EvaTech on Monday," she says.

She holds the letter in front of my face blocking my view of the game. Taking the letter, I scan the contents. "Do I even want to know how I've got an acceptance letter for a job I didn't apply for?"

I turn away from the computer screens to look at her. I know my brown eyes with speckles of hazel look bored at her for even trying to do this for me. Hers are a fierce blue. There are moments when you must admit defeat against the force of my mother.

"I don't need a job. Certainly not one in a company I could run. This is degrading Ma," I say.

"You may have the qualifications to run EvaTech, but you have *no—*" she emphasises the point with raised eyebrows, "—work experience. And, how you got the interview isn't important. You're not the only intelligent one in this household. You will go and you will interview respectfully. End of story."

After my father died, Ma had to become both parents. The disciplinarian and the nurturer. She had to fight silent battles with a moody teenager and rage loud wars with an over-achieving gamer. It took years for me to acknowledge the roles Ma had to play. And although she lost the love of her life, she's been a powerhouse who can now stand here at my gaming station and demand that I attend a job interview I had no knowledge about. The mischievous glint in her eye means that she knows she's winning this battle.

I groan, reading the job position. Executive Assistant to Blair King. Looking up at my mother, I know she has done something to pull this off. How could my mother get me a position at one of the most influential tech companies in the country?

I've spent my adult life doing online university courses, living in the basement of my family home, gaming and making a small living from playing video games and tutoring students. It seems that Monday will be the day that either starts my external working life, or I disappoint my ma. If I don't give this position a shot, she'll know and after all she's done for me over the years, I have to at least try.

Studying and gaming was my way of coping with the loss of my father. Burying my head in technology and books, I could escape this world and emerge victorious in another. I managed to complete a double degree in business and computer science, before completing a degree in communications and an arts degree.

I'm overqualified to be an assistant. Fuck, I could run that place. But I'll hold my tongue. After all, my mother didn't spend years inflicting manners on me, just so I'd throw it in her face that I'm overqualified for the position.

Turning around, I witness what this means to the strongest woman in my life. I can read the hope in her eyes. The pleading to know that I have to at least give it my full attention.

"Enjoy your game, Miles. Come Monday, you'll be employed." She does a little dance and fist pump in the air to show her victory. I just shake my head at her infectious ability to win and make the world better. The force of June Hunter is stronger than any natural disaster.

As someone who has survived on less than five hours of sleep for more than half their life it's been acceptable because I mainly just rolled out of bed to sit at the computer and start my day. But Monday is a different story. I have to look acceptable. Presentable. Professional. I'm the potential Executive Assistant to the head of EvaTech. Over the weekend, I managed to keep my mates busy on the gaming scene and ventured out to shop. I didn't know buying suits for an interview was so time consuming. They measured far too much of my body. Certainly, too close to particular areas.

I investigated EvaTech and Blair King as soon as Ma left on Friday afternoon. Creating EvaTech after ten years in Silicon Valley and from the ground up, her reputation for taking control of the market in app development is amazing. Credit where it's due, she certainly knows her way around an app design.

Ensuring I look the part for the position, in a three-piece suit with colours designed to highlight my features without looking like I am posing for a magazine cover, I make my way to the front door of EvaTech and nervously walk toward the reception desk.

"Hi, can I help you?" the receptionist asks.

The woman is polite as I fumble my way through an intro- duction and produce the letter for the job interview.

Her smile is welcoming but being around people can be a struggle for me. This is more of a test than my mother could've known. In the pandemic years I hadn't met more than a couple of new people face-to-face. The joys of technology improvement meant that everything was done with a screen between you and the world.

Handing back the letter and a lanyard with a keycard on it, she gestures toward the bank of elevators.

"Mr Hunter, you'll need to go to the black door elevator and use that keycard to access it. The doors will take you straight to Ms King's office. Have a nice day."

Nodding and murmuring a thank you, I move in the direction she indicated. Clutching my satchel strap, I'm tense waiting for the next stage of this process. I'm so far out of my depth in the outer world. I'm drowning. There's a ping from my pocket, alerting me to a message.

> MA
> You've got this.

She really is the best. With her in my corner I can't fail. That little message gives me a new boost of courage.

The elevator doors open to a hallway which leads to eclectic panelling around a solid wooden door. It's made from old technologies dating all the way back to letters from the printing press to the modern computer chips. A piece of art history like this deserves my admiration. Staring at the history engrained on the panelling, with every blink I discover new pieces of the past. I'm so enthralled by the design and detail; I don't realise the walls on either side are made of glass.

"Are you just going to stare at the panelling or are you going to come in and start the interview?" The voice from inside the office startles me to the point of jumping and looking around until I spot its source. A piercing set of green eyes stare me down with enough power, that they would crumple any warrior in my Role-Playing Games, or reality.

Taking a deep and calming breath, I push through the doors and come to stand at the front of her desk. My knuckles are white from the pressure of holding the strap of my satchel. I don't know where to look or what to do with my hands. I'm looking just over her head at another technology piece of art hanging on the wall. Her desk is not in front of the win- dows. She's set it to the side of the office, allowing the doors to face the ceiling to floor windows that look out over the city. A view that shows dominance and power. Both of which have me confused as to why I've still not said anything.

Clearing my throat, I say, "I'm Miles Hunter. I'm here to interview for the position of Executive Assistant." *That my mother arranged.*

I hold her stare and a smile is hinting at the corner of her lips. The intensity radiating from her smirk highlights the natural beauty. No work profile or other photo I could find on the internet ever showed this vision—full lips with a blood red tinge, demonstrating the magnitude she has in the industry. She sits behind a glass topped desk that highlights long legs in designer shoes. Every inch of exposed thigh seen through the tabletop is a tease executed to trap any red-blooded male. With the combination of her smile, radiating beauty and exposed thigh, my pulse is beginning to pick up.

How is this possible? She scans my body like a metal detector wand at the airport and I can't take my eyes from her. This is not what is supposed to happen. The stirring in my slacks is a surprise to every fibre in my body.

I didn't come expecting to have this type of reaction to Ms Blair King. All she has done is utter one annoyed question to me. And yet here I stand ready to bow in her presence.

"I know who you are, Mr Hunter." She looks at me directly through to my soul. "This is my company, and I know everyone that walks through the door." She indicates to a chair in front of her desk. "Take a seat and we'll get started."

Lowering my tall, lean, six-foot frame into the business chair opposite her desk, I continue fidgeting with my satchel strap. Thankful I have something to do with my hands.

"Do you have a résumé?"

My nerves are escalating. I hand over all I could produce on the weekend, while I gamed with my buddies and shopped for suits.

"I've a list of my qualifications." Surely other people of my age have full résumés and their life's achievements do not fit on a single page "As you can see, I have several degrees that will be helpful in the position."

Blair holds the piece of paper like its next destination is the shredder and I'll be walking from her office defeated. Her disdain for something so small has me doubting why I'm even sitting here. Long, elegant fingers lightly hold the written parts of my life.

More nervous than I have ever been, I stammer, "I know it's not much. But I could make it work. I am a fast learner and intelligent. I mean, how many people do you know my age that have four degrees?" Trying to make a joke doesn't seem like the best idea based on the look she's giving me. "I need this job. Perhaps a trial, if nothing else."

She smooths invisible wrinkles across the page. "Mr Hunter, you are overqualified as my assistant, which could be dangerous. I am the boss because there is no one better than me to run my company. It is called EvaTech because it will be mine forever."

She gives me a stare which would bring men to their knees quicker than any sword.

"Tell me, and don't lie to me. Why are you genuinely here?" Blair asks.

This was it. The make-or-break moment. Like the line delivered by Colin Firth in *Kingsman: The Secret Service*, 'Manners maketh the man'. Taking in a deep breath, I lowered my gaze as I reply. "I'm here because my mother got me this interview."

The silence falls between us to the point where I can't stare at my lap any longer. Glancing up, there is a small smile across her face again, though this time she has a hidden victory behind her eyes. Licking her lips like a predator who had found its most delicious meal, in this moment the ruthless and unforgiving owner of EvaTech is on full display.

"If you are hired, you'll need to be here at seven forty-five every morning and you'll leave when I ask you to."

Standing from behind her desk, this must mean the interview is over. That's it? Watching her walk from her side of the desk to mine, I rise to meet her stance. Her whole face has secrets and walls keeping her safe. But it's the elegant business way she stands in front of me, holding all the power, that has my blood racing through my body lighting all my nerves. There's a small twitch behind my zipper adding to the confusion as to what is happening right now. Do I have the position or not?

I move my satchel to cover what cannot be professional for any workplace. Clouds are starting to crawl into my mind and add to the uncertainty of the situation.

All I can think about is the perfection of her lips and how much I want this job just so I can spend more time with her.

Extending her hand for a shake, I take her elegant fingers in mine and know there is something there. There shouldn't be a feeling like this after a job interview.

"Thank you, Mr Hunter. I will notify you of my decision," Blair says, "Have a good day."

She releases my hand and returns to her side of the desk. That's it, I'm dismissed? Making my way back down the corridor, I stop at a door before getting to the elevators. Looking in the office, I surmise this must be where I would work. The area is compact, with a phone, two monitors, a whiteboard and message board. Clearly it is bare for her assistant to add the personal touches—not that I know what I would put on the wall.

I'm not a motivational quote person and I doubt a collage of my favourite video games would be respected. I haven't even got the job and I'm decorating the space. I need to leave here. There is nothing more to do, and yet, how can I go home and face my mother with no knowledge of my job prospects?

I may spend my life in the gaming world, but they've given me confidence to go after what I want on the screen and take risks, why can't I take a risk with this?

I turn and extend my stride back into Blair's office. She's on her mobile, resting her forehead in her other hand. When she hears me enter, she instantly hangs up without saying anything and her face is transformed back to the professional, fierce owner.

"I want this job, Ms King," I say. "There is no one else who could fill this role, and I won't be leaving without an answer. Do I have the position?"

CHAPTER 3
BLAIR

Y ou've got to be fucking kidding me?
Hanging up on Juni was a little rude, but I couldn't have Miles overhear any of our conversation. She has never told him that she works in the café. It was one of the stipulations about the position for Miles. Although it was her suggestion, it was on his merits that he becomes successful. However, I was calling her to explain why I didn't think Miles could be my assistant.

He has all the qualifications for the technological side of my business. But I need someone who has people skills and can manage the little and mundane things that I am tired of doing. With the burst of his reappearance and demand for the position, my excitement in hiring this young man has just gone from zero to sixty in a heartbeat. He has no personal qualifications or previous experience. Sure, he has the university degrees, but anyone with a degree knows that half of the time is spent socialising, and the other half is listening to someone to tell you fuck all of what you actually use in your chosen field.

Storming back in here certainly showed that when pushed he just might be able to handle himself in the big league. I need someone who can stand next to me and not crumble if it gets too hard.

I steeple my fingers. "You've said you need and want this job, which one is it?"

I see his bravado leaving a little with every breath he exhales. "Need. And want."

"Mr Hunter, I am a very busy woman, I don't have time for whatever game you are playing right now. Tell me why I should award you the position?" I hold his stare. This small test will help to determine if he can face the scrutiny of the executive members at the next meeting.

He takes a deep breath. "Look, you know that my mother got me the interview. I owe it to her to get the job. My résumé is small, I know that. But I'm more than a piece of paper. I can't go back to her as a failure. I've never failed at anything, and I won't let this be the first thing. Not where she's concerned." His shoulders lower, but his eyes hold mine with a hint of the passion of a competitor.

"I will give you a trial for one month. If at any time in that period you do not perform to my standards, you're out." My smile is replaced with the look that brought men to their knees in boardrooms. His qualifications may say he could run my company but, *I* am EvaTech.

I return my focus to the computer screens in front of me contemplating what tasks I need my 'assistant' to do for the remainder of the day. This is new territory for me. I'm used to doing everything.

Rising from my desk, I decide I may as well start with a tour of the private floor and how the upper levels of the business work. He won't need to know what happens in all aspects of the company; he is only here for a month.

"Come with me. I'll show you your office, other areas, and workings on this level," I say.

Coming around to the side of the desk, I'm thankful for the height of my heels. At five-seven, average height for a woman, heels just make it more powerful when standing in front of a six-foot tall man.

"This is more of a private level. Executive members have access for the times that can't be fixed with an email. However, most meetings take part on the level below where a lot of their offices can be found."

We make our way toward his office which has never been used, and it shows in the lack of decorating. "I know it is bare, this office has never been used. You're free to decorate it how you see fit."

"I thought I was only here for a month?" There's an enquiry to his tone.

"Yes, but no one wants to sit in four white walls for

any period of time. You're not in an asylum." I say, moving toward a door at the back of his office. "Through there is your living space for when you are required to stay late."

I leave him to have a look at the area. It's a simple layout, like a budget motel room; a bed, cupboard, ensuite and coffee making equipment. I step away from his personal space. I still don't know if this is the right move for me or EvaTech.

"There is nothing here that has me running for the hills. Do you have work for me, Ms King?" Miles asks.

That title from his lips is giving me feelings that no man has managed to investigate in several years.

His question gives my mind something else to think about. No one calls me Ms King like that. Most people in the company operate more like a family and just address me as Blair.

"Yes. Please follow me." Being more professional is an easier approach at this stage. Standing around attempting to make conversations is not what either of us are here for.

Getting comfortable behind my desk, I decide I may as well give him the tasks that are always at the bottom of my list. Afterall, he is here to assist.

"I will need you to email the executive team and inform them of your position. While you are communicating with them, familiarise yourself with all their positions and what they are expected to do at

EvaTech. I will need to be included in all correspondence until you have established yourself."

Why is he not taking notes? If he thinks he can remember all the tasks, good for him, but I will not repeat myself.

"I will set up your work email and send through my diary for the next month so you can familiarise yourself with what is expected from you and what you will need to do. All calls will go through your office from now on." I was sure this would be too much for him.

"Is there anything else, Ms King?" He seems confident that he has remembered all I've asked of him.

"No," I say, waving him away. "You're free to go."

It's been five hours of clicking buttons and reading files. Surely, he's settled in by now. Pressing the speaker button on the phone, "Miles, I need you in my office."

Watching him walk down the corridor to my area and through the doors set the butterflies in my stomach alive with a tiny tickle. Not wanting to take a full flight yet, they just let me know that they're gathering to soar up and out.

"Yes, Ms King. You called."

Even that innocent, polite response has my blood sending a little tingle through my veins. What is going on? I've taken out companies. Crushed competitors. Had men quivering in boardrooms. And yet Miles has my toes curling in my Manolo Blahnik heels.

"Are you settled in?"

I stare him down, watching his eyes to see just what kind of person I've hired. There it is—the fiery glint I knew would be lurking under the surface.

"Well Ms King—"

"Please call me Blair. Only when we are with other employees should you address me as Ms King. Otherwise, it will get old rather quickly."

"Okay, Blair. I finished those tasks you sent me and made some modifications. Can I show you?"

Miles begins walking toward my side of the desk. This is not what is supposed to happen on the first day of work. My legs have all but turned to water. I can't move. Thankfully, I'm seated. The butterflies are in full flight now.

He leans across me to grab my mouse and put it on the left-hand side. With his right arm resting on the back of my chair he's leaning down, focusing on pulling up windows. His eyes dart around the screens.

His scent is like a bubble surrounding him, and now I'm on the inside, and all I want is to breathe it in and not leave. It has become my new air. A mixture of spicy and light aromas designed to capture all my attention.

Breathe Blair. Remember breathing, it's important.

I can't take a huge breath of him; it would be too alarming.

I start small—just in and out, in and out.

He turns at that moment, and I'm lost. His eyes aren't just hazel and brown. They're innocent, with a hint of mystery. Sharp angles along his jaw have me clenching my hands to stop from running my fingers along the smooth, clean, unmarked skin. His youth is written all over his features, drawing me in further.

He clears his throat and turns back to the monitor.

"As you can see here, if we cut the fitness app that was developed last year and use those funds to design a completely new app in its place, I believe the new product and its marketing abilities will put EvaTech even higher up the industry ladder. I have an idea for an app, and to my knowledge no one has created it. It'll be the first of its kind," Miles says.

Where has this kid been? In five hours, he's been able to complete my list of tasks and come up with an idea for a new app.

His lips have stopped moving, but I can't take my eyes of them. Just enough volume to feel soft like a feather tickling my ... A sound breaks my wish. Fuck! I was just caught staring at my assistant.

I'm near speechless. I didn't realise I needed an assistant. And I now know I don't. I need *him*. I also need to say something, so he doesn't know about that little daydream about his lips.

"You're left-handed?" I ask the first thing that comes to mind.

He turns. There's a little crease in his brow. "Pardon?"

"You've put the mouse on the left side." I indicate to his action.

He smiles down at me with a youthful cheek about him. "That's what you noticed? I've potentially saved you thousands to make you millions and you ask if I'm left-handed?" His eyes now have a mirthful spark in them. "No Blair. I'm a gamer." His voice seems to have dropped an octave and increasing my body temperature to a passionate scorching degree.

His eyes have changed a little, but it happened so quickly, that I'm not sure if it happened at all. Did he realise that I was just fantasising about his lips mapping my body and wanting more? I want more with Miles.

"I can't believe you've done that. It shows great potential and intuition to continue here at EvaTech." I say, clearing my throat. Hiding my thoughts is not something I'm used to doing. I need space and my own bubble that doesn't have the essence of Miles Hunter in it.

He stands up from my chair. My words seem a little empty without him in my space. He has broken the cocoon. This is his first job, and I need to keep it professional. I can't be thinking about all the naughty and unprofessional things that I could do with him here on my desk. He's only here because his mother wants him to have a job. And I'm his employer, his boss. I can't be seducing or fantasising about the production of the map his lips would create.

Fuck off fantasies and lust. This kid, and the twelve- year fucking age gap, can take a hike. Why did

I say a month probation? That will feel longer than the Hundred Years' War. But those fingers... Neatly trimmed nails, and I've never noticed before that hands could be muscular. Gaming has exercise benefits. No! That's not what is happening here. Every time I look at him, I am finding more things to be mesmerised about. 'Thank you, Blair. I'll go back to my office now." His voice pulls me from the inner turmoil his body and attributes are inflicting on me.

"Actually Miles, I think you've earnt yourself an early mark. I'll see you here at seven forty-five in the morning. Please bring an extra change of clothes. If we're going to discuss the changes you're proposing, and potentially start designing the app, I'll need you for longer hours tomorrow."

"Yes, Ms King. I mean Blair. Thank you."

I catch sight of him readjusting himself as he walks out of my office for the day, and I can't help but smile. It seems that I'm not the only one affected by the proximity of the other person in this office. But he's far from walking out of my life. I shouldn't want someone as much as I want him. And I shouldn't want him because I'm his boss.

CHAPTER 4
MILES

I can feel her gaze boring into the back of me as I leave her office. I have to readjust myself. My dick has never responded to a woman like that before. She's my boss. I can't get involved. But the moan that escaped her lips while I was talking about the new app and the other progress I'd made today bypassed my ears and went straight to my cock.

I add a new security system to my computer, close every- thing down, then grab my satchel. Stepping out into the hallway I look towards Blair's office and there she is, looking back at me. Has she been staring in my direction this whole time waiting for me to remerge from my office? She rises higher in her seat as the side of her face lifts into a smirk. A sexy smirk that would only lead to one thing, and right now I'm not too sure I should be thinking about that.

For the past six years, Blair hasn't had an assistant,

therefore the executives could just come up unless a block was put on their cards. The history shows that has never happened. I'm surprised she has lasted this long without assistance. It is a testimony to her strength, that she hasn't burnt out.

Just another reason why Blair is such a powerhouse and not someone to mess with.

While I was familiarising myself with the executive team, a few flags came across my investigation. Kaleb Morriss seems to have Blair in his back pocket as one of the original team members of EvaTech. Dempsey Sevrick follows all of Kaleb's motions that are put forth in executive meetings. Rarely does he contribute his own thoughts, but he certainly knows coding and programming. Jasper Simons is as innocent as a lamb. His head seems so buried in numbers that if it doesn't have a dollar sign in front of it, he can't function. All the female executives didn't raise so much as a hair on my arm.

Stepping out of the elevator in the lobby, I make my way over to the young woman from reception this morning who directed me to the elevators for the first time.

"Kenna, isn't it?" I ask. I know who she is I just want to show manners. According to her file she is new to this position but came highly recommended from her previous employer.

"Yes. Sorry, I don't remember your name."

"That's okay. I know you're busy with everything

that goes on at the front desk. I'm Miles Hunter, Ms King's new assistant. I sent you an email today just outlining that if anyone enquires about Ms King, I would like to be informed first. Just in case she is busy and shouldn't be interrupted."

"It seems you are taking your job very seriously," a deep, arrogant male voice declares just behind me. "You haven't even been here a day yet and you're already making demands. Does Blair know that?"

I don't have to turn to know who the voice belongs to. I had watched a few interviews he had given for products over the years, and Kaleb Morriss, the Executive Director of Marketing—essentially the second-in-command—has a very distinctive voice. In the interviews and the information I was reading, he doesn't seem like someone you would want to have your back to. His file stated that Blair had hunted him from a big marketing firm that dealt with several companies in Silicon Valley. He didn't need recommendations or references and had come quickly once Blair had started EvaTech.

There was something about his mannerisms and position within the company that rubbed me the wrong way. But, with only hours under my belt at EvaTech and not the years he's had, I can't rock the boat without hard evidence based purely on my gut instincts.

Standing to my full height, I'm a little taller than him. The power trip may be lost on him, but I take great pride in knowing he has to look up to me.

"Actually, she does know. I was just talking to Kenna ensuring she is up to date with the correspondence that was sent out," I say.

I hold his stare. This is out of character for me. I don't normally have this much bravado outside the gaming world. But Kaleb Morriss is someone who holds too much power and it doesn't feel right.

"Just as well." His sneer is evident in his voice. Turning on his heel he walks toward the elevators.

"That man gives me the creeps," Kenna whispers, probably not realising I could hear her comment.

"There is something about him," I agree. "Have a good day, Kenna. I'll see you in the morning."

Just as the sun's rays belt down against my fair skin and attempt to attack my eyes before I can get my sunnies on, there's a ping on my phone—a tone set for my gaming group chat. I read the message with relief.

> LOGAN
>
> Losing the castle, where are you, Millie?

I haven't told my buddies about my new job for two reasons: one, they'd all want to work here and two, they only want me to game and not move from the basement because of how dedicated I am to gaming. I quickly reply.

> MILLIE
>
> I'll be there soon, just stepped out.

I've had the location off on my phone since last night so they can't track me, but these guys are great nerds. If they wanted to find something—or someone, in my case—it'd only take them as long it takes me to get home. I'm grateful for the early mark now, although Blair said she needed me longer tomorrow. I need to be home and secure the castle and the rest of this game.

I don't bother going in through the front door to greet Ma. I don't even know if she'd be home anyway. Straight to the basement, headphones on, I'm ready and saving my online territory just as the enemy starts running toward the gates.

I've been at this for a solid two hours when I notice Ma is walking down the stairs.

"How was your first day?" she asks, coming round to peer over my shoulder at the screen.

I'm sure if she looks hard enough, she'll realise that I've been home for quite some time. There are a few snack packages scattered amongst water bottles around my gaming zone.

"Great. Blair was great. All great," I reply, but I'm in the zone. I don't want to elaborate. Plus, I don't want to think about how easy the work is or the sound that Blair made while I was talking about the new app.

"That's great, honey. Dinner will be ready in thirty minutes." The no nonsense June Hunter takes with her gaming son is evident.

"I'll be up."

Staying focused on the game and putting strategies

in play so I can leave my kingdom unattended tomorrow, I don't realise Mac is talking to me on a private line. "Earth to Miles. You there, Miles? Millie, answer me!"

"What? Mac, what's wrong?"

"I've been trying to get your attention for the last five minutes. What was your mother talking about? Do you have a job?"

Shit. I forgot to turn my headset off. No one was talking, too focused on the battle around the castle.

I can't lie to Mac; we've been through everything together.

We left school early and completed similar degrees.

Checking the connection is on a private setting I reply, "Mac, I have a job at EvaTeach as Blair King's Executive Assistant. I didn't want to tell you all because I know how much you all want to work there."

"Well, I'm hurt. You've never kept anything from me, and I saw you yesterday for our weekly run," Mac replies.

I know he is joking, Mac doesn't hold any grudges, but a little sting at my own betrayal has me spilling more information. "And in all honesty, Ma came to me on Friday night with the job interview letter. She arranged it. It all seems quite suss to be honest. But I tell you man, today was hilarious what she had me do. I had it finished in close to three hours. I managed to figure out a new app and investigate it before she called me into her office to discuss the day. Then she gave me an early mark."

I know Mac is taking it all in—figuring out the best way for me to get through more than one day without telling the rest of the boys what I've done. That's the best thing about Mac, he'll look at all options before speaking. Words are important in his world, and he only speaks when he's sure of the right ones to use. Unless he's with women. That man can have a woman begging in a matter of minutes with a few whispers in her ear. At six-foot-two of long, lean limbs and no fat, most girls get the smile, then the whisper, then naked. His stories have had us all in awe at how a nerd can get the girl. Perhaps it's because every second book he reads are the smutty ones with all the ideas. I trust this man with my life.

"Alright," he says with thoughtful consideration. "We'll play this game in the afternoons only, but if you can't make it, I'll play as a double and the others may not figure it out until the weekend. Will that give you enough time to sort it out this week? After the weekend, I doubt that I'll be able to fool them. I'm a bit pissed you didn't tell me yesterday, but I get it. Don't fret, I've got you Millie."

"Mac you're the best. Do you want a job?"

He laughs. "Not yet. But I'll hold you to it later."

We continue playing until I get the message saying dinner is ready. They all know that if Ma sends a message for dinner, it's time to move. They've been here when she marched down the steps, interrupting our game with more force than a sergeant. My teenage years taught all of us the importance of food, our mothers and manners.

June Hunter is a force and since my father died, it's been just us. It took a few years until I realised how much she needed me, but she never gave up on me. She slowly gave me little life lessons while still ensuring I had my identity in the world. Keeping the lawns mowed to perfection and helping around the house were enough at times to get her through a rough day at the cafe or when she was missing dad just that little bit extra.

Sitting at the table, our chatter about today comes with ease. The moments around the table are worth more than any hours in the basement.

"I don't think I'll be home for dinner tomorrow night. Actually, I don't know how long I'll be away. I've proposed a new app idea that Blair is willing to discuss tomorrow and it may take some time. I'll message you before you go to bed."

She just nods and finishes her meal in silence. I'm not too sure about her reaction. Normally she rarely finishes her meal because she's too busy talking and listening, but tonight there's a difference to her. My social cues are never on par with others, but I know Ma. Something isn't right. I watch her fidgeting with the napkin and pushing her food around the plate. There are stress lines on her face.

"You look a little worried about something. Can I help?"

She straightens and tries to hide the issue that's swimming behind her eyes. "Darling, I know you want to go back to the basement. I'll be fine."

I can tell that's total bullshit. "Nice try Ma. Look, I'll deal with the kitchen. Mac has my back down there anyway." I collect her plate, taking it to the kitchen and pour her a glass of wine. "Here, take this to the bathroom for a glorious bath or go snuggle in Dad's oversized armchair with your book. I've got you covered."

Kissing the top of her head, I hand her the glass of wine. She doesn't even have it in her to argue with me and I know badgering Ma about her problems will not solve them.

Bolting upright and panting like I've just finished a sprint at the Olympics, I have to look around and get my bearings. My heart feels like it's about to explode out of my chest. It was just a dream. She isn't here. She looked real and she was in my room, walking toward me in nothing more than a suit of armour and heels. Her breasts were exploding from the top of the armour, with just her nipples hidden inside. The suit moulded to her body like a second skin. It was like she had just stepped from my game. Blair King dressed as a goddess battle warrior is my new favourite image.

Rubbing my eyes, I look at the clock. I've only been asleep for a few hours and I know I'll never get back to sleep with the replay of my dream weaving its way through my mind and my cock now pitching a tent in my sleeping boxers.

"Genius, I've got a little surprise for you." The dream is so fresh I don't even need to close my eyes to recall the details. Staring into the darkness of my room, I can easily imagine Blair King walking toward me clothed in her battle armour.

Slipping my hand beneath the band of my sleeping shorts I grab hold of my cock with a firm grip. With one pull from base to tip, I hiss with the thoughts of what pleasures her own body could bring mine.

Closing my eyes, the images from my dream of Blair strutting towards me has my breath coming out in pants. Quickly reaching over and grabbing a bottle of lube from the drawer beside my bed, I know this is going to be the quickest and most fulfilling release of my adult life. Covering my cock, it's only minutes before all the images and faces of my past fantasies are replaced with Blair in all her glory. Her commanding voice yesterday in the office, mixed with the sight of her in armour has me quickening my strokes and breath. The pressure is building, starting in my lower body and raging straight towards my hard dick. Throwing back my head in a silent scream of passion with the memory of Blair's moan in the office yesterday, long white ropes of cum land on my carved stomach.

Sucking in deep breaths trying to regain a normal breathing pattern, I know there is no point in attempting to go back to sleep at stupid arse o'clock. I may as well get up, clean up, and get ready for what is likely to be a week at the office, if not more. Reaching the office before seven, I'm thankful for the all-access keycard. I don't have to see or interact with anyone. Making my way up in the black door elevators, I step out and into my office. I go to the extra door behind my desk, into what looks like the budget motel room, and start unpacking all my supplies. Setting everything I've brought from home in the wardrobe, I make my way to the bathroom to unload my toiletries. In here, I can hear what sounds like panting coming from the other side of the wall.

Leaving my office, I walk towards Blair's. The closer I get, the louder and more defined the panting becomes. Being as quiet as I can, I walk behind her desk and continue toward the sound. From where I'm standing, I can see her shadows dancing around the room.

Hesitating to move forward, my dream comes back to me in full force. I must see. I have to know what this woman looks like when she's not dressed for business or walking around in armour in my dreams.

At the corner, half my body is hidden from view.

But I can see all of hers. Dressed in yoga leggings and a sports bra, her fists are wrapped for shadow boxing. Sweat is running down, leaving rivers of perspiration across her exposed skin. With my eyes tracking a line of sweat down her body, I haven't realised that she's stopped boxing and is looking directly at me.

All my blood has left my brain and headed straight for my cock as my eyes travel back up to meet hers. That half smirk is back on her face as she walks toward me. I'm frozen to the spot. My feet won't move. My brain is saying run, but nothing is working, except for my cock. It's the only thing that's moving.

"Do you like what you see, Genius?"

She's taunting me. I can see the mischief in her eyes. It's déjà vu. It's my dream all over again, just in a different attire and setting. Digging my fingers into my palms, stretching the skin across my knuckles, is the only thing that lets me know I'm awake.

Her hips are moving from side to side the closer she gets.

When Blair's standing within an arm's reach of me, I finally find my voice. A small part of my brain is back to functioning mode. "Couldn't sleep. Came early. I didn't know anyone would be here at this hour." My voice is broken. Simple sentences are all I can manage. This is the hardest test to date I've ever had to pass, and I honestly think I'm failing.

Scanning my body, her eyes make their way back to

mine. "It looks as though you certainly do come," she leans in to whisper, "early."

Turning her back on me, I watch her sway her arse back to the workout area, bend to retrieve a towel and walk to what must be her ensuite. Realising I'm still watching her, I feel a small amount of pre-cum leak from my cock. Embarrassed beyond belief, I quickly turn and race back to my own in-house suite to get my shit together before I start my day in the office. She's the boss and I may fantasise about her, but I can't have that interrupting my employment.

CHAPTER 5
BLAIR

Everything that the workout was supposed to get out of my brain just came flooding back the second I saw him. Why the fuck is he here this early?

I didn't go home last night, instead choosing to spend the night in the suite. I stayed here hoping I could clear my head, get more work completed, and be ready for the design of the new app today.

As soon as Miles left yesterday afternoon there wasn't much time not occupied by thoughts of him and what I wanted to do. Attempting to get some sleep I'd worked out before bed to the point of exhaustion, only to be woken a few hours later with the need to drive to his house and entertain the dreams and fantasies of the past twenty-four hours. Instead, I rolled over and pulled my magic wand from the bedside table. Normally porn videos or smutty literature is needed to have my clit throbbing and me screaming my release to the empty building. Last night, all my thoughts were of my assistant and what is hiding under his suit. I'd seen his magic fingers at work on the keyboard and mouse. I'd never thought men in the technology field could bring those desires to my body. With the vibrations playing across my clit, and the thought of those strong fingers in charge of me like his game controller, my pleasure hit me so quickly, and I came so hard, I passed out with the wand still in my hand.

Now, back in the present and my breathing after seeing him here at this hour of the day is not what I wanted. This can't keep happening. Dreaming about my assistant crosses all the boundaries: age gap, office romance, professionalism. If this is going to succeed, having fantasies about Miles Hunter need to stop. I need to focus on keeping my business at the top amongst all the competitors.

An hour later I've had a shower and done basic hair and light make-up. I'm wearing a pin-striped skirt suit with my favourite pair of Christian Louboutin heels. A woman can rule the world with a good pair of shoes, and I plan to rule mine.

Walking from my suite to the office I find a stack of papers on my desk and a hot pot of tea. I take in the sight and a smile crosses my face. Pouring the liquid into my delicate china- ware cup, the aroma surrounds me. I'm lost in the sweet scents wafting throughout the space. This is what an assistant is supposed to do.

Make sure everything is in order for the workday. He said he was a fast learner, and this is the result of that. It was in the information I sent him yesterday that I like aromatic tea in the morning set out to perfection.

There's a light knock at the door before Miles steps through. He's wearing a three-piece navy suit with a tie and lightly patterned shirt which brings out the flecks of hazel in his eyes. And every platonic and professional thought about my assistant has just flown out the window. I've seen men in suits my whole life, but my assistant is at the top of my list. I didn't think I would ever be jealous of material. Slightly rocking my hips from side to side does nothing to relieve me of the feeling building in my core. It isn't even eight in the morning and already I want to lockdown my level and get to know Miles on a more personal level.

"As you can see from the information on your desk, there are a few in-house issues that need your attention before we start discussing the app. Do you have any questions?" His voice redirects my thoughts. His professionalism is what I need.

I didn't really pay a lot of attention to his physical appearance yesterday. Right now, when he shows some authority, intuitive and sex appeal, my legs are starting to squirm a little. It's going to be a long day if I can't control myself at this hour.

"No, thank you. I'll call you when I've looked over these papers and we can start brainstorming the app. Please ensure that we aren't disturbed from nine for the remainder of the day, unless it is an emergency. Do you know how to put blocks and diversions on emails and phone calls?"

His demeanour changes automatically. The professional, light-hearted assistant is gone, and a hard look comes over his features. I can't tell from this distance if he's annoyed or begin- ning to flirt with me. We haven't spent enough time together for me to get a read on the cues in his eyes. "Yes, I know how to do those things."

His voice is abrupt when he turns and leaves my office with an air of annoyance about him. I don't like how that feels deep in the pit of my stomach. He walked in here relaxed and is now leaving with stiff shoulders and a straight back. This is not a great way to begin what will be a long day.

His departure leaves me with an uneasy feeling, but I need to dive into these files so we can start designing the app. He has his directives to complete before we start. If he can't handle being told what I asked him to do, then he can leave. I survived six years without an assistant, I can return to those times. It's only been one day. He may have eased my load in those small hours, but I won't bow to any man.

Huffing out a breath in annoyance that I needed to justify myself, I deal with the files he left on my desk and only hope he is actually completing the daily tasks that have come in overnight.

A little before nine, Miles walks into my office like

he is all business, and nothing happened earlier this morning. His laptop is tucked under his arm. Setting up at a table opposite my desk, he begins to gather supplies needed for a long day of coding and designing. He continues to move between his office and mine setting up the stationery, snacks and a hydration station needed for the day. I'd finished the files some time ago, and was double-checking that we would be uninterrupted for the day.

Sitting at his laptop, everything about his position is telling me that he's waiting for me to come and join him. Granted, he could probably design this app by himself, but he's waiting. It is a sign that he knows who he's working with. I'm excited to be working on an app again.

Grabbing my laptop and going to sit with Miles, I feel we need to clear the air about his departure earlier. If I must sit here all day, I need to be in the right frame of mind and environment to design.

"What happened when you left here earlier? You were all relaxed and ready for the day, then I give you a directive and you get all stressed, tight muscles and grumpy."

He looks up at me, several options of how he could answer the question cross his face.

Taking a deep breath he says, "I'm sorry Ms King. It's just that I'm not used to people not knowing what I'm capable of. I could do what you asked before I left high school." His voice deepens with agitation. Taking another deep breath, he shows me the card I knew he was hiding. Juni had mentioned that Miles is capable in all areas of technology. "I could run your company. I think the easiest thing for us going forward is to have the understanding that I can do everything you ask of me." It isn't arrogance. It's matter of fact—direct and to the point.

He is capable of everything related to the technology side of my company. And although his résumé is light, his knowledge isn't.

The blaze in his eyes as he stares me down is nothing less than powerful.

"You'll never run this company," I inform him, leaning in.

This is not the easy and relaxing work environment I wanted for today. Fuck me, how can I fix this? I want to code. I need to get back to what made me want to start this company.

"I'm sorry. I'm not used to sharing and I'm protective of all that I've built. Can we please move forward and see if we can get this app started?" I ask, setting up my laptop and other papers. "I'm not here to make the place look better." His quick wit has me smirking. He may think he's not here to make the place look better, but in that suit and a half smile, it wasn't looking bad. "You're forgiven. Let's get this happening."

Changing my thoughts from his looks, I say, "You came up with the idea for an all-in-one movie app.

Why?" It has potential and I'm excited to be back in the coding zone.

Fixing all his items he needs for his work area—lollies, water, headphones—the age gap has never been more evident. "Let's be honest, when you want to watch your favourite movie, but you haven't got the streaming service, it pisses you off. This app allows you to watch any movie regardless of the streaming service." He looks at me with an innocence his age carries. At this angle, I can only be his boss. He's too innocent. He just wants his movies.

"It seems like a caring and comforting app. You seem quite passionate about it, Genius."

His eyes fire at that word so quickly. Here one moment, gone the next. Now that is more like the Miles who had enough fire in my office yesterday to demand this job.

"Ms. King," He replies. "I know how to care and offer comfort."

Oh, there seems to be a bit of banter coming from the young man. The cheek. It seems he knows how to rile me up. Crossing my legs and rolling my hips, I try to create a little friction. Those two words can make it happen.

Deep breaths, Blair. Miles Hunter knows the value of simple sentences and direct words. Especially when those words are directed right to my centre. But I put those thoughts aside as we get to work.

Hours later a growl rips through the quiet hum that

has settled over the workspace within my office. We both looked at each other before smiles spread across our faces. It seems my stomach has announced it needs refuelling. Looking out through the windows, the natural light has been replaced with artificial. No wonder the sound broke through. I haven't eaten anything all day. The snacks and hydration station hasn't been touched since it was set up at the beginning of the session. This is the problem of creative juices and loving what you're doing. It's easy to get buried in the joys and excitement of creation.

Miles continues to work as if nothing has occurred. I watch him typing away with fingers flying across the keyboard and his eyes darting in all directions across the screen. He looks at ease, peaceful and like he belongs here.

"Let's go out for a meal. There's a quaint little bar at the end of the street—my treat. After all the work you've put in today it's the least I can offer," I say.

I need to get out of this office, and I want him to come with me. I can't believe I just asked him out for a meal, but I want to know more about this young enigma. He just has a presence about him. I need to get to the bottom of this man and work out my feelings for him in the process.

His eyes still haven't left the screen and it looks as though he hasn't heard me and I'm second guessing if this was the right thing to do.

"Okay. I mean that growl could've been heard

down in the lobby." He doesn't look at me while speaking, but the cheeky smile stretching the opposite side of his face, has convinced me that this is the right thing to do.

I brush off his insult toward my growling stomach. "Great, I'll pick you up from your office door in thirty minutes." I leave him to finish whatever he needs to do so I can go and freshen up.

I shower and swap the business attire for pleasure —a light floral wrap dress and heels. Light make-up and messy bun and I'm done. Limited effort with maximum impact.

I'm standing at his office door when it opens to reveal Miles dressed in a pair of slacks and button-down shirt. Doesn't this man own jeans or chinos? Being a gentleman, he produces his elbow for my hand, linking us together. We work together. I'm his boss. But at least I know chivalry isn't dead.

We step into the elevator and the doors close. "You look lovely tonight. Although, I think you look great no matter what you're wearing," Miles observes.

His shy admission about my appearance puts a spark in my heart and gives me courage to speak about him as well. "I've enjoyed looking at you. Even if it has only been for two days."

We travel the rest of the way to the bar in silence. His arm remains bent, allowing me to stay close to him the whole way. Once inside the bar, it is reasonably busy for a Tuesday evening. The waiter gives us a table at the back, and I'm grateful. I want a little time to just be with Miles and get a gauge on all areas of him.

We order enough food to put the growling monster at bay, plus table wine.

"Tell me, Miles, what type of gaming are you interested in? What takes up all your time when you're not developing innovative movie apps?"

It seems the only way to get this man talking might be his interests. A silence has fallen over the table, and while it might be comfortable in the office, with the sounds of fingers dancing across a keyboard, out in public, it's uncomfortable.

Taking a sip of his wine, his eyes hold a cheeky glint in them again. This time, he doesn't try to hide it. "I play RPG. I have a group of mates that, like me, spend their days inside and in front of screens creating havoc on the imaginary worlds."

Normally it takes more than one glass of wine to loosen my lips, however, the thought of Miles in an RPG position seems to add to his appeal. "And what role do you play in these games?" It's hard to gauge if he's sipping his wine for the taste or confidence. "The commander. The hero. The lover. Whatever I want."

Suddenly, it's hot and hard to breathe. I can't take of a sip of the wine quick enough to moisten the desert that's in my mouth. And his eyes know it. They are loving that the boss has been put in her place in the gaming world.

Trying to regain the upper hand away from the

youthful eyes staring me down, I have to ask a safer topic.

"Why did you bury yourself in so much study if you already had the gaming world?"

"My father died when I was a teenager, and it was just my mother and I." A little wince comes over me at the mention of family. I didn't think this was where the question would lead. "And Ma wanted me to be more than just a gamer. I buried my head in study and found that it came easily so I just kept doing it." Taking another sip of his wine, I can see the admiration he holds for his mother. "It's actually why I want to achieve so highly at this position. I want to make Ma proud of everything I do. I want her to know that I appreciate all the time and effort she's put into me."

He'd been talking more to his hands, so he hadn't seen my reaction about family. That's not a topic I want aired in a restaurant. Mine is one of a troubled past and hidden with the present knowledge that I know about his. I quickly reschool my features before he can lift his head and see the emotions flying across my features.

The night continues to flow with some banter and stories of mates. All too soon our meal is over, and the plates are removed.

The waiter brings over the cheque and Miles reaches out to it.

"What are you doing? I asked you to dinner. You are not paying for the meal," I say, firmly.

His eyes are burning with what must be his 'lover' player looks in his games. Passion and lust are stirring with each other around his hazel-brown eyes. "Please, let me. I've never done this before."

I couldn't hide the shock on my face if I tried. What has he never done before? Too many questions race forward but are congested and choke on any comment wanting to come out. All I can do is nod and remove my hand from the bill wallet.

Walking back to the building and up to our suites in silence, I'm still thinking about his statement. Stopping outside his office and swallowing several times to add moisture to my mouth I finally say something.

"Do you have much to work on? I think we achieved a lot today. There doesn't seem to be much left to do. I'm sure we can finish it tomorrow before the staff meeting that we pushed back to midday," I ramble.

"I'll just finish up a few little things that I thought of over dinner. Thank you for a wonderful evening."

He pats my hand and walks through to his office where his laptop is waiting on his desk, pleading to be opened again and have the keys tickled.

I walk through to my suite, replaying the evening. I wanted him to kiss me goodnight. I wanted to kiss *him* goodnight. But the professionalism I've instilled must be followed. I go to my fridge and grab a glass of wine then pace back and forth across the carpet barefoot.

With the bottle of wine nearly empty, I can't stand the absence any longer. I have to go to him. I'm still in my dress from dinner. Softly walking through my office, I decide not to use the hidden door between our suites. I make my way out into the hallway. The glow from his office tells me that he's still there. At least I know he's dedicated. I want that dedication in the bedroom as well.

I stand in the doorway, but he doesn't even move as I hold the door open. "Miles," I say, in the most seductive voice I can muster, "why are you still working?" Walking around and sitting on the edge of the desk, I reach out and stop his hands flying over the keyboard.

His breath hitches at my sudden touch. He lifts his eyes to meet mine.

"I'm nearly done." It comes out in a broken whisper.

Miles expertly flicks a few more keys while his eyes stay on mine. I slowly lower my mouth to his and give him a featherlight kiss. His eyes close and a moan leaves on a whisper. I haven't pulled all the way back. I want to see if he has the intuition to continue this.

Rising slowly, he stands in front of me. He lowers his head to my forehead, resting it there. His breath is laboured, like every intake is using all his energy to stay standing. Strong, gaming hands rest lightly on my hips. It was just a kiss. It wasn't supposed to be this strenuous. He's at war with himself. I can feel the uncertainty within his body as to what the next move should be.

"I've never done anything like this. I want you, but I've never failed at anything in my life, and I don't want you to be my first failure," he whispers.

Fuck. This is the lack of experience he was talking about. How can I possibly turn down that confession? How can you get to twenty-six and not have had sex? This is unfathomable to me.

I'm thirty-eight and now the age gap seems too big to breach. Fuck, I need to put the brakes on this. But everything about this man has me telling society to go fuck themselves. He has my body on fire where his fingers are lightly resting on my hips and after the feather kiss and his admission, I want him more. I want to be the one that ensures Miles Hunter does not fail.

Reaching up to cup my hands on either side of his face I lean into his lips, lightly kissing them again I pull back enough to whisper, "if you don't want to continue this, tell me to stop now. Otherwise, put your hands under my arse and carry me into your bed. I'll give you the best lesson of your life. And I guarantee you won't fail."

CHAPTER 6
MILES

Following the instructions, I lift her off the desk. Her legs automatically wrap around my waist. Her arms twine around my neck, keeping her lips close to mine.

Should I kiss her? I'm not an expert at this. In high school there were a few stolen kisses and a few touches under clothes hidden away in the shadows of library stacks or dark corners. This is nothing like that. This is a woman. My cock is standing at attention. It feels like electricity is running through my bloodstream and every step toward my bed, I feel my cock growing harder.

This is nothing like my dream last night. I've spent my life living in a fantasy of the gaming world. Reality is far more rewarding. Everything about this moment is nothing gaming has to offer, and Mac could never have described this feeling flowing through my body.

I'm a virgin, but I never expected to find a woman that could pitch a tent in my pants to this height. I won't be able to touch her without blowing my load and embarrassing myself. I know it. My mind is racing thinking of everything except the feeling of her lean thighs in my hands. My fingers have a mind of their own as they slowly massage and knead her tight, athletic arse. I've no idea what type of underwear she has on, but it doesn't cover much of her sweet cheeks.

Taking deep breaths, all I can smell is her rich summer flowers scent. It has sporadically tickled my nose throughout the evening. This close to her, it's all I can breathe. It's the only air I need. Her eyes are hinting at the anxiety I'm feeling. She leans in to rest her forehead on mine.

"It's ok. Just breathe, Genius. You can do that, can't you?"

The sassy glint in her eyes at challenging me lights a spark from my toes and travels up through every fibre in my body. This woman. If she's going to test me, she better be prepared to lose. I never back down from a challenge. I'm a gamer. I win everything.

She knows I won't back down. Looking straight in those mis- chievous eyes, I say, "Ms King, don't challenge me. I guarantee you won't win."

Feeling the muscles on her thighs contract at the same time as her quick intake of breath, I've discovered that calling her Ms King is going to help me later. I let my smile light up my whole face. Her breath is starting to pant when I reach the bed and lower her to the covers.

With my knee between her thighs, I sit back to remove my tie and start unbuttoning my shirt. She sits up and places a hand over mine, stopping me in my action.

"Allow me."

Coming up on her knees, we're face to face. Her expert hands undo every button with ease and precision. Reaching the bottom, her hands travel up the defined ridges of my torso and reach my shoulders, to push the material off me. I haven't removed my cuffs making my arms trapped by the sleeves.

"Leave it like that." Her demand is whispered yet holds more power than a roar from a drill sergeant.

With the lightest of touches, she pushes just enough to have me walk backwards. Using her mouth and little directions, she's able to manoeuvre me so we've traded places. I'm now standing with my back to the bed. With just one sharp fingernail, she presses at my shoulder, and I fall to the mattress. Bouncing back up, I finally settle on the covers, trapped and at her mercy.

Crawling up my body, she straddles my thighs and lowers her lips to mine. She runs her tongue across my lips and they instinctively open, allowing her access. Our tongues become acquainted. Light strokes teasing for more. With my arms trapped in my shirt, I can't hold her. She's loving the power of this situation.

Breaking the kiss, she lifts her head and smiles down at me. "Don't come until I tell you."

Why does she keep making demands of me? Fuck, she's discovered my weakness: challenges.

I can't stop the moans escaping with every action and attention her body is giving mine. I'm aching with the need to touch her. Reaching my trousers, she starts undoing the button and zipper. Her eyes are focused on me. Challenging me not to spurt my load all over the bed. I won't close my eyes. I'll stare her down like the vixen she is. She won't win.

"Lift your hips," she demands.

I can see how this woman is the head of a massive tech company. She can command attention and set demands with the smallest amount of volume from her perfect mouth.

She leaves my trousers around my knees. Fuck, she is locking me down with my own clothes. I can't move anything more than my hips. I watch as she lowers her mouth and blows on my cock, now at full mast. The pain in holding back from that small action has me writhing. Her hands are holding my hips to the bed.

"Remember what I said, Genius, don't come." Lowering her mouth to cover my long, thick, veiny cock I hold my breath and watch as she brings herself back to the tip, before giving it a little suck and popping it from her mouth. I think about anything other than the beautiful woman between my thighs. Deserts. Reading Latin. It's not working.

I don't care about my shirt. I rip my arms free. All the passion and pleasure she's building in me is giving me Hulk- like strength. Reaching down and grabbing her from my cock, she pops off in surprise.

"What the fuck are you doing?" she asks.

"Sit on my face," I say, pulling her all the way up my chest. I have no idea where that thought came from, and I don't care. "You've had some fun. Now it's my turn."

One lick along her wet slit and I'm nearly coming from her sweet taste. Every time I flick my tongue across her clit, Blair grinds harder on my face. Loving her responses, I take note of her actions and follow what she wants.

I slide a finger in her tight pussy, and her moan is echoed around the room. Pumping in and out of her while sucking on her clit has her juices running down my hand and into my mouth. She tastes better than anything I've ever had or anything I will ever have. Blair King is all I want to taste.

Grinding down hard on my finger, riding out her pleasure, the scream of my name ricochets around the room. Both of us are sucking in deep breaths. I'm still as hard as granite and I don't care. The woman above me slowly comes back to earth after the orgasm I milked from her body. I've heard a woman's pleasure should be given before your own. Right now, the person who gave me that information needs a medal.

Seeing her blissed out in the aftermath, gives me more satisfaction than any other accolade.

Slowly, Blair regains enough strength to climb off my chest and move down my body.

Her face hovers above mine. Licking inside my mouth gathering all her essence, she says, "Mmmm, you taste like me." "I like that taste," I say, as her hips start to rise and fall, dragging her pussy along every inch of my cock. Teasing me. "I may need it again very soon." My voice is husky with lust.

Humming into my mouth, she says, "it's my turn now." Kissing, nipping, sucking her way down my torso, she stops at my hips. Never before has my cock been so hard. Full, straining and reaching to get any touch from her. Blair takes teasing bites, her mouth dancing from hip to hip, never touching the one spot I need her to. My breath comes out in hisses and pants.

Pre-cum leaks from my cock. Blair, licking at it threatens to have the whole load following her action. "I could get used to this taste, Genius."

That nickname. It's the start of my undoing. "Jesus, Blair, fucking suck my cock. Or I'm coming into thin air."

She lowers her mouth taking me deep into her throat. Pulling back, she's kissing me again with long agonising strokes of her tongue up and down my shaft. I know I won't be able to hold on. It's a miracle I've lasted this long.

She increases her speed, creating a fog in my brain

so thick I've forgotten what it was I'd asked. Panting and tossing my head around on the bed I hear the sweetest sound.

"Come for me."

Releasing the pressure, my toes curl and I throw my head back and roar as I unload what feels like my life down the back of her throat. Watching, she continues to milk me with her hands and mouth, sucking every last drop from my body. Creating pleasurable twitches and nerve spasms as the last of my load runs into her mouth. She licks it up, rises from my cock and begins to kiss her way up my body. Hovering over me, looking deep in my eyes, she smiles down at me.

"That's a pass in my book Mr Hunter."

CHAPTER 7
BLAIR

My body is still humming from the orgasm and pleasure we've just given each other. Moving up his body, I slam my mouth to his. Tongue diving between his lips as they open in surprise at my sudden action. Swapping tastes as our tongue's dual for dominance.

Rolling to pull him on top of me, I continue kissing him deeply. Breaking the kiss, I can see a little uncertainty in my virgin. It seems I'm going to have to give him a bit of a tutorial. And love every moment of it. I'll train him to worship my body.

"Suck my nipples and breasts. Taste every inch."

Miles begins the trek down my throat with light kisses and nips. Every time his mouth leaves my body, I'm craving its return. Every touch has electricity sparking at the spot and spreading out, traveling around my body.

Fingertips trace every rib on one side, while his other hand massages my tit. My nipples are hard peaks. His teeth grazing the sensitive points has moans of pleasure escape me. "Yes, Miles. Right there."

My pussy is wanting in on the action, but my chest is taking all his attention. And it's glorious. Miles takes instructions and responds with enthusiasm. My body is so alive it's like the age clock is going backwards.

"Miles," I say, lifting his head from my breast, "I need more." I rub my thigh against his hard cock. "Fuck me."

"I haven't got a condom."

The innocence of this man is baffling. He can control my body with his tongue, teeth and mouth, but the moment I mention I want to fuck him, his innocence has me thinking this is not what he wants.

"I'm clean and I can't get pregnant,' I say, "if you don't want this, we'll stop right now." Cradling his face in my hands, I lightly kiss him in understanding. "Just go at your own pace, I'll match you."

Placing himself between my thighs, I open a little wider. I'm exposed, fully on display and although he's licked me out to the point of a mind shattering orgasm, it feels different, more intimate. His feathery touches along my pussy lips and to my clit are more personal and sensitive than any other action. He's studying my responses to his caress. Following my body and the reactions he's drawing from his touches.

Slowly inserting two fingers, the stretch is

unbelievable, I'm so wet there is no resistance. My back arches off his bed, moaning.

"Look at me." His demand is strong. "I need to study how your body reacts, so I know what I'm doing. And I want to see you come."

Using his thumb against my clit, I'm twisting in ecstasy. If this is what it feels like to be high on passion, I want this feeling daily. Why has no other man asked this of me? But my little virgin assistant, wants my undivided attention. Fingers moving in and out of my pussy, it isn't long before another orgasm is barrelling through my body heading for a release.

Just as the first tingle of release comes across my body, Miles removes his fingers and replaces them with his hard, throbbing cock.

Our moans fill the whole top floor of the building. We match each other thrust for thrust.

"Fuck, Blair. Come baby. Squeeze my cock. Own me." Scraping my fingernails down his back, he hisses at the pain.

His thrusts become more erratic. He smashes his mouth to my nipples and bites and sucks the pleasure right to the surface. Throwing my head back, I scream out a second more powerful orgasm.

My pussy milks every ounce of cum from his body as his roar of pleasure is matched with mine.

Together we slowly come back down to earth after pure fulfillment. The feeling of our combined release sliding down my slit. It should be gross and uncomfortable, but it has the opposite effect. I want more of it.

Sitting back on his knees, Miles lifts his fingers through our juices. "What do you want me to do with this Ms King." He swirls it around my overly sensitive slit, waiting for my directive.

"Whatever the fuck you want."

Cocking his head to the side, like his processing my answer, thinking of the best outcome. He inserts two fingers into my pussy and, pulling out, our juices are coating his fingers.

Lowering himself toward my mouth, I'm panting again with anticipation of what he has in mind.

"Lick it." He holds his fingers at my lips, waiting for me to follow his command. What I didn't expect was for him to lick the other side as my own tongue flicked out along his digit. "Good girl."

Moaning around his finger, I didn't realise that those two little words would trigger another wave of passion.

Waking up in the arms of my assistant was never on the bucket list. The light pinks waking the world, spill around the blinds in Miles's suite. I feel safe. I want more of this. And more of last night. Flashes come back to me with every blink of my eyes, creating a movie of images like my own personal flipbook. I contemplate facing the world or closing my eyes to relive last night's pleasure. I opt for the latter.

Hours later, with the sun directly filling the whole suite, I'm still torn between what's right and what *feels* right. He feels so right. He felt so right last night. The way he ate me out. Licking me from arse to clit, sucking lightly on my centre, then spearing his tongue into my pussy, while his fingers worked more magic from every corner of my soul. And that was just the starters. I've no idea where he learnt it. But that man was able to read the pleasure in my body better than previous lovers. His source of knowledge needs to be given to all men, so no woman is left unfulfilled.

I peel myself off him a limb at a time. I am still his boss. This is still my company, and although I don't give a shit what the employers of EvaTech may think of an office romance after two days, it isn't really the look I want for the business. Looking down at him, breathing lightly through his beautifully kiss- swollen lips, I make my escape.

Tiptoeing out of his suite, I make my way to mine. I bypass the need to exercise to clear my head. I doubt my body could handle more physical activity anyway. Five rounds of fucking with multiple orgasms last night has certainly left my pussy in need of a rest and my legs feeling worse than after running a marathon.

Walking in to stand under my full rain showerhead, the water is warm enough to loosen some of the stiffness in my unused muscles. I haven't pulled an all-nighter like that in more than a decade. His stamina has my mouth twitching into a smile with the memories that continue to swim through my mind at a leisurely pace. Lowering my head so the water cascades down my body and thinking of the pleasure that came from last night mixed with the uncertainty of the future, I'm deep in thought when the warmth of the water is taken from me and replaced with the warmth of a body. I'm familiar with every inch of that body after my exploration last night. With one hand holding my hands to the wall where I'm resting, the other is snaking around my body to slide down my stomach and slip into my folds.

"Good morning, Ms King. You weren't in my bed when I woke. I had to come and see if you were okay." His fingers massage the nub of nerves at the apex of my thighs. His digits glide in and out of my entrance with ease. I'm wet again.

A wanton whimper comes from deep in my body as I'm throwing my head back onto his shoulder. There are no rational thoughts going through my mind. All I can register is the pleasure that these young, strong fingers are pulling from me. Finding my voice amongst the pants of pleasure I ask, "how did you get such strong fingers?"

A deep growl of laughter comes from the base of his chest. "I told you, Ms King. I'm a gamer." He knows licking the outer shell of my ear and hearing him call me Ms King will send me over the edge. I press further down onto his palm and ride out my orgasm.

Releasing my hands, Miles catches me around my middle before I collapse to the floor of the shower, knowing my legs feel like they're made of rubber after another mind-numbing orgasm. He pulls me back into his torso, and I stand, panting, and try to remember what I was thinking about before the amazing interruption. I don't want to get caught, or trapped in these strong arms, but it's hard to deny the comfort and security they're offering.

Taking a deep breath in, I spin around, looking up into his youthful, hazel-brown eyes. I blurt out, without thinking, "we can't tell people about us." What was I thinking? This is my company, and we have a twelve-year age gap and he's my assistant of less than forty-eight hours.

Looking into his eyes, I expect to find heart ache and rejection. Instead, all I see is understanding and compassion.

Holding my gaze, Miles lowers his lips to mine and lightly kisses me. With the shower still flowing all around us, it's like we're in a cocoon. Just us. Just this moment. No outside world. No multibillion-dollar company that needs our attention. In here, I feel like I've made a mistake, that we could be an *us*.

"I know, baby. But let's add a 'yet' to the end of that statement, shall we?"

Oh Miles, why do you have to be everything I want

and more? If I tell you what I know, you will run. And I don't want you to run. I want you to stay.

Lowering back down and removing my lips from his, I can feel the tingle of his kiss and the understanding in his eyes as it all unfolds. I can't look in his eyes much longer. After what we shared last night, the secret of his mother working for EvaTech in the café and the only reason he got this job was due to her asking more like a favour, is weighing on me more than the weight of the world. The innocence of his life with be obliterated if it comes out.

Keeping my voice quiet, barely above a whisper I place my hands on his chest, "Miles, we have a lot to do today. It's Wednesday, which means a staff meeting and the morning working on the movie app. Let's get ready."

Grabbing my loofa and applying the shower gel, I start to spread the soapy fragrance all over my body, with my eyes closed. I don't need to look at Miles, I just need to escape back into my head and reorganise my priorities.

Feeling his strong hand, cover mine he says, "let me."

How could I say no? Nodding, I release the loofa into his hands and feel every ounce of my body cover in goosebumps as his hand ghosts over mine and traveling around every inch of me.

This feels like a fairy-tale. Like a hero is coming to save me, and bring me back to life. No man has ever taken the time to know my body like he has. Normally they're either after my money or pleasure. He seems to want more. And I can't give him that.

Altering my thoughts and priorities, Blair King, the owner of EvaTech, needs to walk out of this shower and own her life. Once we're out of this suite and in professional mode, no one will know what happened behind the office doors last night, or in the shower this morning.

Miles and I are all professional as we pass each other with nothing more than boss and employee demeanour. We sit in meetings discussing the progress and developments of my company. At times, I can feel Miles glancing at me. Our gazes catch each other unaware. Memories fly between our looks, that are quickly hidden from the rest of the team members.

The marketing team, headed by Kaleb, are asking for access to the new app with all the information.

I look towards Miles, to gauge what Kaleb has just asked, but he's giving me nothing. Taking the lead on this, I state, "I think the best way forward with this app is to launch it at the start of the month, in two weeks' time. It's not finished, but a prototype can be used for marketing with employees and a closed BETA testing group. That way we can determine if there are any glitches, ensure it's targeting the correct demographic, and find the correct approach to all areas of the market."

Watching Kaleb take the information, he gives

Dempsey a quick nudge. "I'm with Kaleb about the new app. It's a brilliant idea. But, perhaps I could take a look at it as well. Add my coding expertise. No app has ever left EvaTech without my input or complete design."

Acknowledging Dempsey's input, he's not lying, but this is mine and Miles' design. Quickly glancing at Miles, he's still giving me nothing. "Dempsey, you can have what I give Kaleb. But no changes can be made to the code without the approval from Miles or myself."

Everyone around the table in the conference room turns and start talking to the others around them. The atmosphere is electrified with the addition and small presentation about the movie app. The teams are looking through what we already designed, talking over how it may unfold. I can hear the chatter about the app and I'm proud to have been able to contribute more than just thoughts to the whole code situation with it. I've missed the hands-on approach to my company. Being the boss, I know all about the apps and programs we've developed, but there was always a longing to get back into the designing aspect of it all.

I risk a quick glance at Miles, who's standing just behind me. There's something about his look that is not sitting well with me. It's like he's frozen but trying to remain professional and hidden while his eyes translate for his mind what looks to be going a mile a minute with unknown thoughts.

Quickly schooling his features, he pulls out his

phone, nods to me and is out the door. What the fuck just happened? I want to follow him, but Patricia needs to talk to me about more HR aspects of the company that I can't get away from. This day is turning into a whirlwind. The bliss of the morning has quickly been replaced with the demands from Kaleb and Dempsey and now HR. I really need to go home tonight. I know if I spend another night in my suite here, I'll be more inclined to go to Miles' bed and not mine.

Every moment throughout the day when we exchanged glances, I wanted the memories of last night to become a reality again. But I have a company to run. He is my assistant, and I know as soon as he discovers how the position became available after six years, I'll be back to an overworked owner and an empty bed.

CHAPTER 8
MILES

It's times like these I'm glad of two things: one, no one knows me so I can just blend into the scenery; two, the ability to follow my gut and have people on my side with the skills I need. Because after the presentation and listening to Kaleb and Dempsey, something is not right. There's a twisted feeling living in my stomach at the body language and behaviours on display in that meeting.

Although I've only spent one amazing night, and two spectacular days with Blair, I'm not about to let someone I care about get hurt, and that's the vibe I got a moment ago in the conference room when Kaleb and Dempsey spoke about the new movie app.

In the elevator I hit Mac's number, and he answers on the second ring. "What's up?"

When you've been through as much as we have a phone call holds more weight than a message.

"You near a computer?"

"Soon, just wait."

In the middle of the afternoon, you never know with a gamer. They could be going through a bender, just waking up or outside getting the minimal amount of vitamin D needed without having to take supplements. While waiting on the phone for Mac, I settle into my office and get things organised from my end.

"Ok man, I'm at my station. You alright? You sound worried."

"Mac, I need you to do two things for me."

I know I'm talking fast but I need this done before Blair walks past my glass walled office.

"Go Millie, my fingers are poised."

"Firstly, look over all information on Kaleb Morriss, Executive Director of Marketing at EvaTech. Second, I'm sending you the code and app that Blair and I created yesterday. Send it to the gamers and ask them to go over it and trace its path. Find any glitches, advantages and benefits to it. It's top secret."

This may get me fired, but I trust my buddies more than anyone inside EvaTech. If there is something wrong with the app, they will be able to find it. If I lose my job, so be it. I may let Ma down, but she'll get over it. Once all the glitches and benefits for EvaTech come through, Blair will forgive me as well. It's worth the risk.

Together our fingers are flicking across the

keyboards creating a cacophony of taps and music that only a tech head can appreciate.

Mac is the best hacker, coder, and man I know. He's been contracted at times by several agents to track and trace people who have been living off-the-grid for years. He's able to send the agents to their door with flowers and been rewarded handsomely for his service to the nation. It's amazing what he's been able to achieve in his mother's basement.

The ping of the elevator has my fingers pausing over the keyboard.

"I need to go. Message me." I hang up. I begin rearranging my screens, just in case Blair walks in.

Hearing the click of her heels in the hallway, she seems to be lost in her own thoughts. It's all power and strength as she strides pass my doorway focused on her destination.

Everything about her is radiating a force that can't be stopped. Her mind is going a mile a minute and her feet are on autopilot. It's both disturbing and mesmerising to see her like this. The mighty woman who has brought businessmen to bow before her, has me in awe of her talent and capacity. But the woman from the last twenty-four hours seems to be hidden behind the power coming from her, and I want that back.

I hear her heels stop just inside her office. It's like she's just realised she's in there and her mind doesn't know what to do or why she there's.

Rising with my tablet in hand, I carefully walk around the desk. Standing at my door, I look towards her. My assessment is correct. I see her turning from side to side attempting to judge exactly what she needs to do, waiting for her mind to catch up to where her feet have brought her. It seems the stress of the meeting and everything is catching up with her. Even from this distance I can see the tightness in her shoulders.

Deciding this is not an assistant's duty, I quickly turn, place my tablet on the desk and walk to her.

Lightly placing my hands on her shoulders, I begin to rub her worries away. I can see her visibly start to relax and unwind. Centre herself. She needed this. Blair needs more than an assistant right now.

Kissing her hair and continuing to massage the stress and worries away, she leans into me, and I drop my hands to wrap around her, pulling her towards my torso. I bend down and lift her up into my arms, carrying her bridal style over to the chaise lounge in the corner of the office. Sitting down, I cradle her close to my chest, making sure I'm still caressing parts of her body. Finally, she raises her head from the corner of my shoulder and neck.

The afternoon sun is muted by clouds adding to the mystery feeling of why Blair is acting like this.

"Why did you walk out of the meeting? You had a mysterious look on your face." Her whispered concern for my behaviour warms my soul.

I kiss her forehead and work my way down her face

to her lips. "Don't worry about me baby. I'm not that good around people I don't know." Hiding the feeling about Kaleb from her is eating at me. "What can I do for you? What do you need?"

I know what I want to give her—more of last night. Just to focus on her and every inch of her body and mind. I want to take all her worries away with my lips, tongue, cock.

I won't disrespect the spectacular woman cradling in my arms. I'll find the problem that seems to be floating just below the surface in this place. Something is not sitting well with me at EvaTech and I'll fix it for her. Then she'll know that when

I say I can run this company, I'll do it with her. I don't want to be at the helm alone, I can only be a better person with her beside me.

"I can't stay here tonight,' Blair says. "I need to go home. I know I told you to pack for a few nights and you are welcome to stay here if you have work to complete. But I can't be here right now." She goes to stand, but I hold her close a little longer. I need a few more moments to make sure she's right to leave, knowing she is not going to be here tonight for me to look after. "You have to let me go. I need to finalise a few things before I leave."

"No. I don't want to let you go. Not yet." *Not ever.* I kiss her softly. It's too early to say the rest.

Normally something like this only happens in the movies. But as the thought continues to swim around my overactive brain it holds more weight than anything else. Blair King could be the one and only woman in my life.

She relaxes back into my shoulder and starts playing with the buttons on my shirt, sliding her fingers into the small opening she created. She begins crawling her fingernails over my abdomen. My cock fires to life. I've managed to keep it under control while comforting her. Yet, as those fingernails leave little grooves in my skin, I can't control the sensation and electricity flowing straight to my manhood, now tented and trying to wedge itself between her thighs.

"Ms King, what do you want?" There's no denying what those two little words do to her. I found out last night what it means for her to hear her name between pants of pleasure. She just walked in here all dazed and worrisome though. I can't jump her on this lounge. Although her fingers are doing a fine job of erecting my cock to full mast, it's all about her and what she wants. Obviously, my head and body are working against each other. My body wants this, to lie her down and fuck away her worries. My head wants to soothe them away, but if she keeps working those fingernails over my abs, my body will win this round.

"You know exactly what I want. You gave it to me last night, and this morning in my shower." Leaning in to kiss along my collarbone, neck and jaw, leading to my mouth, she whispers, "give it to me, Genius."

That's it. That's the word she knows I can't refuse.

Grabbing under her arms, lifting and spinning her around, I almost throw her to the lounge in my rush to be back inside her. I can't help it. Hearing 'Genius' is like waving a red flag at a bull. All I want to do is rip everything out of the way to get to her core. Get to my Blair. I need to be inside her.

Her breath is coming just as fast as mine. I don't even have time to strip her skirt or panties away. Scrunching her skirt up to her waist, pushing her panties to the side, I feel how wet she is with one swipe of my finger along her slit. Lifting the digit to my mouth, I suck her essence off. There's no resistance as I thrust all my inches in as deep as they can go in one smooth movement and cover my mouth to hers. Both of us whimpering at the taste of her on my tongue. I want this woman to realise that no matter what she says, I'm not going anywhere.

"Fuck me, Miles. Own me in this moment."

"Yes, Ms King." The innocence of those three words matches the pounding that I'm pouring into her sweet channel. How have I not known that women held this secret? Pure bliss of pleasure that can't come from anything other than the tight, internal muscles of a woman's pussy. However, there is no other pussy I'll ever want. This is all I want. All I need. Blair King. She's it for me.

Watching the sun dance across the office and brighten her green eyes has me falling harder for this beautiful, intelligent, powerful woman. Blair arches her back, and I know she's close. It's one of the tell-tale signs from last night. I change my angle a little to make sure that my thick veiny cock is rubbing right over her bud of nerves.

"Yes. Fuck. Yes." Every word is panted out with the electric pulse of my thrusts into her dripping, tight pussy.

Throwing her head back she exposes her elegant neck, and I bury my face there. Sucking. Nipping. Biting. Adding to the pleasure my hard dick is creating, bringing her closer to tipping over the edge into ecstasy.

Her glorious channel is tightening around my cock as her orgasm takes over her body and I'm right there with her. Releasing another load into the most beautiful woman in the world. Her light brown hair is starting to fall from the high ponytail that's normally all poised and in place. Her lipstick is slightly smeared, with a freshly fucked look coating her flushed cheeks. She's never looked more gorgeous.

Staying connected with her, I reach down and around to gather her close while our muscles begin to relax and stop the spasms from our combined orgasms.

Lightly kissing her face I ask, "you okay, baby?" I can't let her go.

But she has other thoughts. Nuzzling into my chest, she begins to remove herself from around me and I can feel the emptiness that her absence is creating. I have no choice but to let her go, even though every fibre in my body wants— no, *needs*—for her to stay.

Rearranging herself and standing from my lap. She looks down at me, sprawled with my thighs open and her elegant frame positioned between them. "Miles, I'm going home."

Her statement hits me in the centre of my chest with no room for argument or clarity. These are the words of Blair King, ruthless businesswoman and owner of EvaTech.

Watching her gather her things, it's a robotic action. Why does it seem like she's having doubts? She doesn't even look back as she walks from the main office toward the black door at the end of the hallway. At the doors of the elevator, I've finally found my feet and am standing at her office door when she looks up. Just as the elevator doors close, a single tear runs down her cheek. And she's gone.

CHAPTER 9
BLAIR

Walking into my apartment on the western side of the city, I can't believe how my life has changed within a week. And it's all because of Miles. That man has done everything and more. My whole body and soul is torn in too many ways to count.

My head knows this is wrong. There's a twelve-year age gap. He's lived a life of innocence in his mother's basement. A life through a screen—a fantasy, no reality—with his buddies and online gaming.

My heart wants every inch of him. Inches being the descriptive word. How could someone with so much to offer a woman in the bedroom get to twenty-six without using that amazing appendage. He followed my moans and instructions while I directed him around my body until he was giving me what I wanted. He became a master of playing my body. It craves the tingle and the touch that he gives. The featherlight kisses, to the passionate, consuming ones. The caressing touches to the encompassing hold of his nimble fingers.

I can still feel all that he has given me even now, when I'm back in my home. It's like he's been made for me. He knows what I need, how I need it, and all without directives.

Everything is telling me yes. Except my head. And that's the challenge I need to overcome.

Falling onto my bed from all forms of tired, I curl up hugging a pillow, wishing it was Miles. I brought this apartment for the sunset views and peace and quiet away from the city. Right now, I'm too exhausted to look at the view and my head far from quiet with thoughts of Miles.

I wake feeling drained as I look out at the city in the distance. The skyscrapers stand tall reminding everyone of all the wealth being made and held within their walls. For me, it's a realisation that for the first time since starting EvaTech, I can't go into the office today. Miles will have everything covered, and yet I can't even find the motivation to send him a message. Is this a test for him or for me? Do I want to leave it all to him to see how he'll act without me at the helm? I'm depleted from the whirlwind of the week I've had.

From the staff meeting last week, hiring Miles, realising his full potential and the staff meeting yesterday when he stormed out and the executive members were questioning our app design, I have nothing left in the tank.

Standing alone in my kitchen I open an app to order breakfast. I don't even bother looking for food, I know there won't be any. My place is only clean because Florence still comes once a week.

My French toast with bacon and maple syrup is going to take twenty minutes, and as the silence and loneliness settles around me, it's in this moment I need to vent. Looking down at the list of contacts in my phone, the sad reality of the situation is I only have one name in my list who is not professionally or medically linked to me. She picks up just before it goes to message bank.

"Hey Blair, you alright?"

The sweet sound of Juni has a sob locking my throat, making me mute. I don't why I'm nodding. She can't see me. The kettle finishes boiling and I'm making a pot of tea when I finally say, "Nope, but I will be." Those four words come out pained and forced, trying to keep it together so I don't break down over the phone.

"Oh, this sounds like more than a phone call type of conversation." I can hear her clanging around, possibly making her own pot of tea. "Give me the cliff notes version and we'll go from there."

I pour the boiling water into the pot to allow the flavours to brew. I have no idea where to start. This shouldn't be a conversation you have with the mother of the man you have feelings for.

"Juni, I've wrecked it. Everything. Miles truly is too qualified to be my assistant. We designed an app together and it just felt right. Everything about him feels right. Yet I'm hiding out in my apartment because I can't be at the office with him." My voice becomes higher and faster as the words and confessions spew from my lips.

"I know my son, and he has a heart of gold. Stubborn to fault but manners worthy for royalty. Although, I don't think we can truly solve your problem over the phone. It'll be ok. How about you come over for lunch? We can solve the world's problems with good food and great company."

Knowing that Juni Hunter will be diplomatic for both sides, I nod. Realising she can't see me, I stop and smile for the first time since leaving the office. I'm feeling lighter and more capable with her suggestion of good food and great company. "Yes. Ok, I'll be there. Send me your address and I'll be there at one-thirty."

My breakfast arrives surprisingly fresh and hot, and I sit on the balcony taking in the sunshine and allowing the breeze to cover me with a peace I haven't felt in ages. Granted, my mind is still running a million miles an hour but at least my body is here still and calm.

After spending the morning at home avoiding my phone and its notifications, I've read a book, done some online shopping, and placed a grocery order. Being in my apartment, I realised I've missed the simplicity of being away from the office. Pulling up at Juni's house, each step is taken with trepidation.

This could go either way. At least Miles isn't due home until closer to five. I doubt I'll still be here at that hour.

CHAPTER 10
MILES

She didn't come in today nor has there been any correspondence. I can't believe it. It has taken all my effort not to call, email, or drive to her apartment and be with her.

I couldn't have done that even if I wanted to. Between working more on the movie app, getting it finalised for development and release, and essentially running EvaTech while the main chair is empty, I haven't had two seconds to rub my hands together.

I've had Kaleb from marketing enquiring about the movie app and proposing promotional ideas. Jasper from finance has been emailing spreadsheets, figures and projections for stocks, asking that Blair get these and report back to him if there are any discrepancies with the numbers. Dempsey has emailed nearly every hour on the hour about changes he wants to make to the app. I've shut down every single one of them. But he is persistent. It's days like these I think, how the fuck did Blair do all of this for six years without an assistant? I nearly need an assistant.

Mac hasn't got back to me yet, I'm not sure if that's a good thing or not. If we go off the premise that no news is good news, then at least I can focus on the continuous train of emails that ping up on mine and Blair's account.

I know I'm not supposed to clock off before four-thirty, but if I don't get back down underground and in front of my screen, I feel like I might explode. I need to reset after a day at having to deal with all the information that is coming across my desk. I know I signed up for this job, but it's hard to go cold turkey on my previous life. I need to slowly wean my way from the controllers. But the darkness and fantasy of online gaming is calling me.

I also need Blair.

Yes. If I must be above ground, I want to be with her. The office and my life are so empty without her. It's not just her sweet pussy that I want. It's her heart. Her mind. Her body is just a bonus. The night we had dinner, I had a hard time trying to find her fault. Trying to figure out why it can't happen. With the dedication and determination, she put into creating EvaTech, I knew I had to show her my work was a unit she could measure me on. She didn't seem interested in me outside of work-related topics at dinner, but then we had sex, and that turned everything around.

I know if she's not in the office tomorrow, I'll be knocking down her apartment door to get to her. I can't spend another day away from her.

Setting the office up for my departure, re-directing emails and messages, I leave the office by three.

Making my way home, I'm lost in various thoughts about the office, Blair, gaming and life. I walk in through the front door and hear laughter coming from the kitchen. Half in a haze, I recognise my mother's laugh. It doesn't come that often, but when it does you know it's one you want to hear all the time. Ma laughs with her whole body and its infectious. There is no escaping her happiness once you are in that bubble. The other laughter sound is sweeter and lighter.

Rounding the corner to the kitchen I freeze. Sitting at the small table where all my meals have been eaten over my lifetime, I see my mother and my boss. Blair King is in my kitchen, and she's laughing with my mother.

"Oh Miles, you're home early. I didn't know if you were coming home at all tonight. Come and sit down." Ma, rises and begins to pull out a chair for me to sit at the table. There's a pot of tea between the two of them with an empty serving plate that has crumbs from some homemade slices on it.

The only two women who are part of my life are

sitting at my kitchen table having a chat like they're old friends. Something isn't adding up. "Sorry, but what's going on?"

In the confusion of seeing Blair King sitting at the kitchen table with my mother, I nearly dropped half my swearing vocabulary on the conversation. But I quickly stop and close my mouth on that one. Ma never accepts cursing in the house. It's why at times, when all the gaming mates and I are in the middle of a battle and all the colourful language is being flung around, she needs to leave.

"How about you have a seat, and we can tell you what's happening." Ma's sweet sound is trying to calm my racing heart as the seconds continue to tick pass, my frustration of not knowing is growing.

Still standing, I turn between my mother and Blair.

"Who is going to tell me what's going on?" The annoyance with the situation is coming out in my voice.

Blair looks between the two of us and rises. "I think you should sit down and listen."

"I don't want to sit." I shout at them, thankful that I didn't curse. I know my mother has no problem giving me a light clip around the ears to remind me of my manners. She's even done it to Mac once or twice when he's been here.

"Fine. We'll all stand then." Trust my mother to say something that would've normally made me smile

—even laugh— but something is going on and I'm too tired, highly strung and very concerned as to why the woman I am falling in love with is in the kitchen with my mother.

Fuck. Does Ma know that I've slept with Blair? Does she know that Blair is the only woman that I'll move heaven and earth for?

My mother starts as all of us are now standing around the kitchen table. "I've been working with Blair for about five years in the café on the third floor. I know we don't need the money, which is why I only work in the café for a few hours a day, three days a week. About three years ago I personally took her order, and we just clicked. From then on, we'd have a tea or smoothie every now and again and just chat. I love you so much, but I knew you couldn't have been happy down there in the basement, wasting your talent. So, I asked Blair to give you an interview as a favour."

She stops talking and it takes some time for my mind to arrange all the information she's just dropped. I turn toward Blair to see what she has to add.

"Miles, I created my assistant job for you, for the kindness that your mother has shown me. There were days when I just needed to vent to her, and I knew it was private. But I never knew I needed more than an assistant."

"What do you mean, 'more than an assistant'?" My mind is all over the place with the fact that the two most important women in my life have known each other for three years. Ma has never mentioned Blair or working at EvaTech. She only ever said she was working at a café and would sometimes bring home leftover slices and pies. "You've both kept this massive secret from me. I don't know if I should trust anything that comes from either of your mouths."

Half an hour ago I wanted to hear any declaration Blair was going to make but do I want to hear it now? How can I stand here and have this all play out in front of me? Without a word, schooling my features so I don't give anything away after the initial shock of seeing them together, I turn and walk down to my basement. Down to my safety net.

I can hear the murmurs of them talking, but I can't determine what either one is saying. Hearing the front door open and close some time later I still don't go upstairs. That's it. I'm done. My heart has just walked out the front door and I've no idea what I should've done. Right now, I know that I need my buddies. I need Mac. And I need gaming. That's always been my constant. My escape.

Normally Ma would ask if I wanted dinner. Sure, I would sometimes cook and share the load, but after that revelation I just need my gaming friends. I had forgotten just how amazing this group of guys are. We're all different, but together we're one. And they've never misled me like I was today.

I look out the small window and realise I've been playing all night.

I can't face Blair yet. Ma on the other hand... she may be upstairs, and I need to eat. Unlike the others online, I don't have any snacks down here anymore. It's Friday and I'm not going in today. I need to sort my life out. I enjoy working, that's for sure, even though I didn't think I would. But can I really go back to work for Blair King?

At the top of the stairs, I hear Ma in the kitchen and think there's no time like the present to face whatever this is.

Taking one look at my dishevelled clothes the same ones I was in yesterday when I came home, she states, "I know you've been gaming all night. I guess you're not going into work today." "No Ma, I'm not. It's not because I can't, I could shower and be ready in fifteen minutes. I'm not going in because I don't know if I can look Blair in the eyes. I have to look you in the eyes, you're my mother. But I don't know if I'll be returning to EvaTech."

Nodding, she continues in the kitchen, then puts a plate down in front of me, kisses the top of my head, and walks out of the room. Well, I guess that's it. She's not going to give me a lecture, advice, or guidance. She's actually going to let me figure this one out.

All weekend it's been just like old times, which feels like a lifetime ago, even though it's only been a week.

Of course, Mac knows about my job, but the other guys are not commenting about my week that was. Instead, we're hanging shit on each other and living our gaming lives.

It has been a full weekend of chatter about the game. The jeers and banter that is passed around has been at an all-time high and I've loved every minute of it. Although, every time there was a lull in the banter or we're waiting for the action to kick off throughout the game, long legs, light brown hair and the glittering eyes of Blair King would bring another memory to the forefront.

The beauty and the curse of hindsight is that you have a chance to realise just how much you have fucked up. However, the flip side is how do I fix my mistakes? Over the weekend I managed to patch things up with Ma. However, Blair was off topic with her. My apology to Ma was cooking her favourite foods and taking the time to watch her classic movie. It was torture to sit through *Sweet Home Alabama* again, but it's what I had to do to win my way back into her heart.

Blair is another matter.

Everything that happened with her was so fast paced the whirlwind of our time together is still spinning around my head. I know how I feel, but she's never expressed those same feelings towards me. Plus, there was the huge secret she held over me that whole time. Why couldn't she tell me about Ma? Ma had said that she didn't want to mention her relationship with

Blair because she wanted me to establish my own connection with the head of EvaTech.

Swirling around the whole issue with Blair, is EvaTech and not being present to finish the investigation that I'd started with Mac. He still hasn't said anything. Not that I could really protect Blair and EvaTech like I want to, but I did want to know if my hunch on Kaleb Morriss was correct. And the app. That was my first design and creation of an app. It was a buzz that I'd want to recreate or at least see to the end.

My phone pings with a message.

MAC

Meet me at the park in 20.

This is it. He's found something—I know he's found what I suspected, and I'll need to tell him everything. I need to tell him about Blair. I log off and leave the basement, not going through the house.

There's a light wind chilling the air, lifting leaves and letting everyone know the seasons are getting ready for change.

Sitting at the same bench we've conducted all our business at over our lives, Mac is already there with a look that can only be described as victorious on his face. Of course, I've seen this look before, but I don't think I've ever seen it this big.

Reaching inside his pocket like a spy on a blockbuster movie, he hands me an envelope. We do enjoy the theatrics in life at times. Looking around to see if we'll be spotted, I turn it over and pull out the information. At the top of the card in Mac's doctor style scrawl is, *"WE WIN!"*

Those two words are always on the top of our victorious correspondence. Smiling, I continue to pull out all the information that reveals everything Kaleb Morriss is.

I have enough information I need to take to Blair and expose Kaleb. Yet, I'm still sitting on the park bench with Mac contemplating my next move.

"Millie, I didn't just hack into banks, foreign businesses and the dark web for you to sit on a park bench. Take that to your woman and sort your shit out." The thing about having a best mate is they have no filter and will tell you what they want, regardless of how you feel or if you want to hear it. "I know she means something to you, otherwise you wouldn't have made me do all this investigating. What are you so scared of?"

Having an emotional discussion with Mac, it seems like I should be laid out on a couch, not sitting in a park. I give him the quick notes of it all. "Now that I've had this feeling, I want to keep it."

Mac is smiling, and a little laugh escapes his tightly pressed lips. "Millie, Millie, Millie, most of us love our *first*, but how do you really know that she is the one? That she is the love of your life? You've only had the one woman. You and I have had gaming benders longer than you've been with Blair King."

Searching deep into the explanation of feelings it comes to me straight away. Turning to Mac with all the honesty in my soul, I reply, "because my heart knows without her, I am less."

"Then why are we still here?"

CHAPTER 11
BLAIR

I've spent the past weekend at my apartment and its surroundings rediscovering what I love about this place. The museum had a great exhibit on feminine artistry and the depiction of the female body in all its glory. Finding a hole- in-the-wall selling French crêpes was a delicious discovery that gave me an idea for a new app, which I jotted down in my phone to take back to EvaTech. Long walks in the park and along the waterfront gave me the energy rejuvenation I didn't know I was missing.

Exercising inside is adequate, but the feeling of moving outside is something that doctors should prescribe. My soul lifted and every fibre blossomed. My creative tank was being filled with all my new sights and experiences from over the weekend.

Waking this morning, I'm excited to go into the

office and hit EvaTech with all these new ideas, but there's a six-foot-tall, lean assistant who crossed my thoughts during my quiet times or excited moments over the weekend.

The memory of our time together played through my dreams at night. While walking out and about, couples brought

Miles to the forefront again. Laughing, holding hands, stolen kisses. I didn't realise that I wanted it. But EvaTech comes first. The one constant in my life. The reliable source that brings me happiness. I was never lonely at EvaTech. Maybe *alone*, but it wasn't until Miles walked into my life that I even felt those emotions.

There's been no correspondence from him, and I don't know what to make of his radio silence. I didn't expect the scene on Thursday in his kitchen. Juni truly is a beautiful person and I'm thankful I've got her in my life. She's sent me a few messages asking how I'm going, not giving too much away about Miles.

I miss him. His presence is what makes my world go round. Sitting here in my office, I'm not sure if he will come in. He's had the weekend and all I keep doing is looking at the clock, but it feels like it's going backwards. If he doesn't come back today, I'll have to let him go. I will bury myself in work and there'll be no room left to focus on him or anyone else.

I glance at the clock for what seems like the hundredth time this minute. It's eight and he's not here. Lowering my head in defeat I know I have my answer. He's not coming back. Seeing me in his kitchen Thursday afternoon seems to be all it took. The betrayal on his face will be forever etched in my mind. I can't unsee those images. Unhear those words.

Sucking a deep breath in, I straighten up with shoulders back. I'll get through this day, the next and all the others after that. I'm Blair King and I am the queen in the tech industry. I don't need a man to stay at the top.

Too focused on the screen in front of me, I don't hear the ping of the elevator, or the rush of feet coming down the hallway until they stop directly in front of my desk.

I jump, my heart ascending into my throat in full force. I raise my eyes to see Miles walking around my desk to get to me. He crashes his lips to mine. His tongue taking up residence in my mouth, both reacquainting themselves with each other.

Pulling back only far enough, Miles rests his forehead to mine, eyes closed. He doesn't say anything. Just rests there breathing deeply, passionately, forgivingly.

"You're late," I say in my most powerful voice, wishing for him to open his eyes so I can look deeply in them.

"No baby, I'm right on time," he says with a cocky smile.

I have no idea what he means.

His cocky attitude is something that's cute in the bedroom, not the office. "What do you mean?" I need to regain my business power composure while I am waiting for Miles to answer the question.

I notice someone else with him. Any butterflies in my stomach at having Miles in my bubble with his intoxicating scent and mischievous smile are turning into demanding wasps, wanting to know who he's let into my sanctuary.

"Who is this?" I ask Miles, before turning toward the intruder. "This is a private floor, young man. You are not authorised to be up here. Get out now before I call security."

Miles is practically bouncing around. His youth has never been as evident as it is right now. Going back around to stand next to the man, they look like cover models for a nerd magazine. Miles is dressed like he owns the world— a three-piece suit, muscles filling it out, all being highlighted by the glint in his eyes. The other is dressed in a casual style of chinos and a turtleneck sweater that is identifying all his lean muscles.

Gathering my thoughts, I arrange myself at my desk. Leaning my mouth on templed fingers to hold the feeling of Miles on my lips, I glare at both of them, waiting for my assistant to answer my questions. He's late and I'm not sure we can still work together, no matter how sufficient he is at his job and in the bedroom. This is my company and my life. I'm the queen. The goddess. And EvaTech is my domain.

"This is Mac, our saviour. I think we should give him a job. I had a feeling last week about Kaleb, and that's the reason I left the meeting—to contact Mac."

Nothing would be registering on my face. I've spent years perfecting my poker face. I can bring men to their knees in a boardroom and hold them there with a stare.

Knowing I'm still waiting for the real information to be given, Miles continues, "Mac was able to discover that Kaleb has been slowly embezzling from EvaTech and is creating his own company from this company. He was never caught by his last employer and you head-hunted him before his dishonesty could be uncovered. In the time that he has been here, he has slightly modified some of your apps and taken money and assets."

Slowly rising from my chair, I move to stand in front of my desk. This is something that shouldn't have a desk between us. Leaning on the front of my desk and crossing my legs at the ankles, I fold my arms across my chest so that I look more professional. I can't let these two know that I'm fuming and horny at the same time.

"I'm guessing you have a plan?"

Mac steps forward and I notice he's holding a manila folder. "Yes Ma'am. This is the plan to send the bastard to prison and ensure that everyone gets what was taken from them."

Looking over the plan Mac has put together, I still feel in complete shock at their findings. I trusted Kaleb. He was great at his previous company. Everyone was positive about his character. I feel like such a fraud.

Looking up at Mac and Miles, I quietly whisper, "how did you know? I mean, how did you get this information?"

Miles seems reserved, like he's torn between being my assistant or my lover. This news is taking all my energy. My poker face is slipping. He must be able to see the uncertainty across my features.

"Well," Mac starts, dragging my attention away from Miles. "Millie rang me last week and asked me to dig. I have access to a lot of agencies around the world because of my side jobs."

I smile, which seems like a foreign concept when there's a mole in my company and is slowly taking me down, but I can feel the comradery between these two.

"And he was right,' Mac continues. "I found hidden accounts in several offshore banks and other places. There were even fake name accounts, but still linked to him. A pseudonym is easy to trace when it's an anagram. For a clever man, he's quite stupid." Laughing at the simpletons of this world, Mac is shaking his head. Although judging by the intelligence coming from this young man, even a genius would seem stupid to him.

Mac isn't finished. He is getting great delight out of this discovery. "But the real thing that tipped him over was when you and Millie—"

"Stop calling me that. Jeez, Mac." Miles is looking at me with uncertainty. We still haven't discussed where this relationship is going. What relationship we have; professional, personal, both. I just wish I knew what I wanted. An assistant or a forever.

"Oh Millie, she loves you."

I can't hide my shock at Mac's declaration.

"Anyway," Mac seems to continue without a filter like we are all friends in here discussing the latest technology crazes and not the fact that my company is in danger. "When the two of you developed the app, Miles put in a tracking code. It's rare, but I've taught this legend well. I was able to track who Kaleb sent it to and so much more. He actually copied most of the code and sold it on the dark web."

"What the fuck?" That was it. That was the final straw. I'm fuming. Breathing heavily. Opening and closing my fist at my side, I am ready to march down to Kaleb's office and punch his lights out. How dare he take what we'd developed. All I can see is a haze of red in front of me. I am so angry I haven't realised that Miles is standing in front of me rubbing my arms.

"Breathe, baby. It's okay. We've got him. Blair? Baby? Breathe for me. I need you to breathe."

His softly spoken, caring words work their way through the fog in my brain to reach me. Refocusing on his glorious, hazel-brown eyes, I lean my head on his. Inhaling his scent begins to calm the storm raging through my system.

"What do you mean we've got him? He has the code. The app. Am I done? Everything I've worked for—it's all gone."

"Blair, when we built the app, I put in a tracking code, and it can't be replicated. I did it when we came back from the restaurant. The app doesn't work without it, or at least it won't work until I release it. I'm sorry I kept that information from you."

Folding my arms in between us, holding onto the lapels of his jacket, I look up into his caring face and I have to ask. I have to know. "You did all of this for me?"

Laughing and smoothing my ponytail along the side of my head, he rests his strong hands on either side of my face. "Mac was right. Blair, I love you. Forever isn't long enough for me with you. However, I'll cherish every remaining minute of this lifetime to ensure we have eternity."

Grabbing Miles at the back of his head I bring my lips to his. Opening my mouth for our tongues to begin their battle of supremacy, I take his breath and replace it with mine.

"I'll just let myself out. You two have a lot to catch up on." Mac is laughing as he leaves my office.

Breaking from the kiss I move my head around to look over Miles' shoulder at Mac as he leaves. Miles' lips don't leave my neck as I mouth a thank you to Mac before focusing back on my assistant. My man.

"I love you." I whisper in his ear while his lips are trying to cover every inch of my exposed skin.

The three magic words make him pause in his actions. I can feel his lips forming a smile before he raises his head to look deep in my eyes. It means I must have said the right thing. I reached his heart. He's not going anywhere unless I'm with him.

Bending down, he grips the back of my thighs and lifts. My legs automatically lock around his waist. There's power in wearing a skirt in the office, and paired with silk stockings, they give easy access to my core. It's not a surprise that his cock is hard and pushing into my wet panties.

Walking through to my suite, Miles lowers me to my bed. He begins to rediscover my body and I'm struggling to breathe with all the desire coursing through my system.

"Fuck me, Millie." I say, giggling at his nickname.

"No fucking way. You can call me that in the office, but in the bedroom, I'm your Genius."

Miles strips me bare and then it's his turn. There's something sexy about watching him remove his shirt and leaving his suit slacks on.

Moaning, I say, "I want all of you, Miles. Millie. Genius. Give me everything."

Smirking he lowers himself and pushes his slacks enough to reveal his long, thick cock. Reaching between us I guide him to my dripping centre and feel everything fall into place as he buries himself deep in my core.

My orgasm is racing to the surface. I've never come this fast, and I've never felt like this with anyone. Miles Hunter started as my assistant, but he'll finish more than that. He'll be my everything.

EPILOGUE - FIVE YEARS LATER

BLAIR

EvaTech continues to grow from strength to strength and it's only been with the help of Miles. His title remains Executive Assistant. I've asked him if he wanted to be a partner as he practically runs the company alongside me anyway. He allows me time off when I've needed to recharge my batteries. But he said no to being a partner at EvaTech and left it at that.

With all the shit that happened with Kaleb Morriss, more came out about Dempsey Sevrick as well. It seems the two truly were as thick as thieves.

Kaleb was arrested and continues to rot in jail with Dempsey beside him. The executive team were shocked at the discovery but quickly realised that working in tech or any industry, there is always someone bigger or better than you. That little shake up boosted their creative vibes and helped to increase EvaTech's production and stock.

Logan Trembley, a gaming buddy of Miles', now fills Dempsey's role as the Coding and Programming Executive.

He's more than qualified, but like Miles, he doesn't want to run EvaTech—just make it better for everyone.

Elektra Augustin applied for Kaleb's position from Silicon Valley, and it was the right fit from the beginning. Of course, Mac couldn't help himself running a background check. But he didn't tell me until after he found nothing on her.

Miles finally asked if his gaming friends could apply for jobs at EvaTech and they have become some of my most dedicated employees. They continue to surprise me with how they've adapted to life above ground. Although there are times when all of them are back in their gaming worlds.

I'm sitting in my apartment, which became *our* apartment after Miles moved in when his trial month finished. The comfort of wearing nothing more than a tank top and panties on my day off whilst sipping my tea is one I enjoy a lot these days. The sun is setting, changing the heat and bright rays of a late spring day into the cool darkness of the evening. Miles is due home soon and my warm tea is keeping me calm waiting for his arrival. We still spend nights at the office, but there's a new comfort in the previously empty feeling of my apartment. Hearing the front door open and keys being put in the bowl, I know I don't need to move. Miles will find me. His body is so tuned to mine he could find me in the middle of a night club, blindfolded.

"Hello beautiful." He leans down to kiss my upturned face searching for his lips. "You do anything exciting today?" Picking me up he cradles me in his lap kissing my neck before settling into being just with me.

He's in his slacks and bare feet. His sun-kissed, warm torso giving me strength to answer his question.

"I did some shopping." Reaching behind me I pull up a jewellery box and open it to him. Enclosed are matching wedding bands with computer codes embedded in the design. Looking deep in his eyes, the surprise is evident. We may have danced around the point for the last five years, but it feels right. Juni has accepted there won't be any grandbabies. And this is all that's left.

"Marry me, Miles Hunter?"

"I believe I'm supposed to ask you."

Cupping his face, giving him a light kiss and staring into his eyes, I have to tell him. "Miles, I didn't know I needed an assist- ant, but there you were. I didn't know I needed a life partner, but you've filled that role as well. You're my heart. My soul. My reason to get up in the morning."

Staring at each other for what feels like an age, he finally gives me his answer. "Yes, Blair King. I will be your husband." Slipping the ring from the box, I place it on his finger. He takes the matching one and slides it onto mine.

"Yours looks a little bland." He pulls a ring box from his pocket and opens it to reveal a princess cut emerald surrounded by black sapphires.

Happy tears are building and threatening to spill down my cheeks. Everything in this moment is perfect. Kissing passionately, tongues sliding against each other, I rearrange myself to straddle his lap and rest my throbbing core against the tent in his trousers.

"Take me to bed, Genius. Let's celebrate this special moment."

"Yes, Ms King. Whatever you want." "You. Always you."

He lifts me off the balcony seat and carries me into our bedroom to celebrate everything that is special in this world.

ACKNOWLEDGMENTS

Every person who has inspired me since I thought to start writing could be in this list. Some are still in my life; some were never more than a meeting or a smile in the street. But I've cherished all and thank you for fuelling my creative dream.

Firstly, my beautiful friends, near and far, take the number one spot. You've seen me through this journey from the first scratching of pen on paper until long past the printing and now in a reader's hand. You've read every version of my works and that is the amazing thing. Even when I didn't know what was happening on the page, you continued to encourage and support me. Thank you for being with me.

My publishing coach, this printed work became to fruition because you believed enough in me to help and guide me on my journey. Let the rest of my works find the world readers. I am grateful that you came into my life when you did and that you can handle the language and accents that flow from my mouth.

My editor, well you're worth your weight in gold, eat more! From my breakdowns to accepting your praise and discussing the constant changes, you were able to help me turn this seed into a flower. I'm in awe of what you're capable of doing.

My cover designer and rugby lover, your talent and understanding are amazing. Thank you for creating something better than what was in my head.

And saving the best for last; you the reader. If you've made it this far, I truly value that. Thank you. If there's something through my words that speaks to you; a laugh, a dream, brilliant, I've done my job. No matter where you are on your journey, stick with it.

Stay tuned, there's more to come in this series.

Tess, xoxo.

ABOUT THE AUTHOR

Tess Molesworth grew up in a small country town in NSW, and now lives not far from there.

A lover of life, writing, and spending time with close friends, Tess' superpower is her infectious laughter that leaves you wanting more.

Tess is a compassionate and ardent dreamer who is always willing to tell you a story, and can be found crafting them in her favourite local pub.

ALSO BY TESS MOLESWORTH

Coming Soon (2025)

The Apprentice

The Designer

www.ingramcontent.com/pod-product-compliance
Lightning Source LLC
LaVergne TN
LVHW091559060526
838200LV00036B/904